A throne in peril. The crown challenged…

Born of love and hate, King Biryn must fight between the two. The demons within surface when the woman he loves is abducted by his great-grandfather, the fallen god, Zohmes.

Zohmes wants the throne. His abduction of Cylena ensures that Biryn cannot beget an heir. Imprisoning her in Yanata, the underground world of Ierilia and his to rule, he thinks he is one step further toward the throne and the surface.

Biryn must now face the biggest quest of his life, to defend his throne and crown. He has to travel to Yanata to rescue Cylena. With his team, his family, and the help of the god Izarus, he descends to the heinous bowels of Ierilia.

Will they be able to save his future queen? Can they defeat Zohmes once and for all and bind him forever to Yanata?

Testing the Crown
Crimson Realm Chronicles Book 5
Copyright © 2018 Taryn Jameson and Gabriella Bradley
ISBN: 978-1-4874-2054-3
Cover art by Angela Waters

Published by eXtasy Books Inc or
Devine Destinies, an imprint of eXtasy Books Inc
Look for us online at:
www.eXtasybooks.com or www.devinedestinies.com

TESTING THE CROWN

CRIMSON REALM CHRONICLES BOOK 5

BY

TARYN JAMESON AND GABRIELLA BRADLEY

DEDICATION

Taryn Jameson -

To my sister, who sparked my fascination with all things fantasy. We will meet again in the realm of dreams...

Gabriella Bradley –

We are having a blast continuing this series. It has become quite the rollercoaster ride! To our readers...

CHAPTER ONE

Cylena was in Zohmes' clutches. The somber mood in Biryn's chambers hung heavy around his dining table. They expected him to eat breakfast at a time like this? He pushed his food around on his plate. He couldn't keep his mind off her and what she had to be going through. Guilt plagued him. She was so naïve, so innocent, and to be suddenly spirited away by that fiend? He should never have left her and should have fought the lethargy that had attacked him and stayed by her side. Anger gnawed deep within, hatred for the entity that had placed a sleep spell on him, killed Raollin, and had captured her. Sadness overwhelmed him for a moment at the death of his personal assistant, his friend for so many years.

"Biryn, you must eat. It will not help Cylena if you starve yourself," Brenn said, interrupting his thoughts.

He flung his fork, sending it clattering onto his plate. "We should already be in Yanata searching for her! Why the delay? We should go now!"

Astiana, sitting next to him, patted his arm reassuringly. "We need to go to the Clyss first, Biryn."

Biryn took a deep breath to try to curb his impatience. Cylena needed him now and all he met with was resistance. "What could we possibly need at the Clyss?"

1

Ciara answered. "Before we can go to Yanata, your powers must be restored. For that, we need to go to the Clyss. Only the god Izarus, the one above all the gods and goddesses, can do so."

Biryn jumped up, sending his chair crashing back. "Powers? What powers? I never had magick."

Astiana stood and clasped his hand. "Oh, but you did, grandson. You are descended from the gods. Zohmes stripped you of your powers when you were an infant."

Biryn picked up his chair, slammed it into place, then sat back down. Astiana returned to sit beside him. *Gods, so many secrets.* How much more information about himself and his family was hidden from him? He was still trying to get used to the idea that she was his great-grandmother. "Why did I not know about this?"

Ciara gave him a sympathetic look. "Rania has only told Astiana and me about this now. Only the gods and goddesses knew. You have not really needed your magick, but you are getting ready to go on a dangerous quest. You will need your restored powers to complete it."

"It also requires four of us, with the help of Izarus and the goddesses, to transport us all to Yanata," Icaras told the king.

Biryn rubbed his forehead. "By the gods, I would not know how to use it."

"We will teach and help you," Astiana assured him.

"Will we be able to call out our lions when we're there?" Ivran asked.

"Yes. You will," Ciara answered.

Erica snorted. "I feel left out. Three lions, two dragons, a sorcerer, and two sorceresses, and now Biryn will have powers, too. All I've got is a magic sword."

"You have a lion at your side to protect you." Laro kissed her on the cheek.

2

"You forgot me. And I do not even have a magick sword." Aldis grinned. "I requested fleet weapons for all. They arrived a little while ago. We will also each have a long-range proton phaser. They are larger than our hand weapons, but they are much stronger. We do not know what we are going to find in Yanata."

"Probably fucking gigantic monsters, maybe an army of them," Erica muttered, eliciting a giggle from Ciara.

"Should we take some of the engineered soldiers with us?" Brenn asked.

Ciara shook her head. "No, not possible. They are not human and cannot be transported to Yanata."

"So only ten of us will be going," Ivran stated.

"We might be only ten, but together we are a mightier force than any army you can imagine," Astiana told them.

Taylith arrived, his sword strapped to his back. He had left the party early and had taken Tomas and Kira back to Brenn's estate.

"Morning, everyone."

"Have you eaten, Taylith?" Ciara asked.

"Yes, thank you. I have arranged for more protection for Kira, Tomas, Reana, and Issa. I have called in the help of several of my dragon friends. They are already at Brenn's estate and will watch over them while we are gone."

"Thank you, Taylith. That makes me feel better." Laro breathed a sigh of relief.

Aldis stood. "Now that we are all here, I suggest we fetch our packs and get ready to leave." He turned to Biryn. "I also requested fleet uniforms and boots for you. You cannot go with us dressed in your night clothes, or royal attire."

Biryn looked down at his clothing. Because of the upheaval, he had forgotten that he was still wearing his nightclothes. "Oh, yes. I will be fast."

"Would you like someone to help you get dressed?" Brenn asked.

Biryn, already on his way to his bedroom, turned. "Brenn! Do you really think I cannot dress myself? I am quite capable."

"Sorry," Brenn murmured and smiled.

Aldis looked at Ciara, Icaras, and Astiana. "There are fleet clothes and boots waiting for you as well. Please go and change into them. Same for you, Taylith. We will be taking mostly dried foods with us. The kitchen staff has made packs for us containing fresh food that will last maybe two or three days, but as you all know, food will not stay good for longer than that. We need to be cautious with water. I doubt we will find anything edible or drinkable."

Biryn returned quite fast, his sword strapped on and a backpack slung over one shoulder. "I am ready."

"The rest of you, go and get changed and get your things," Aldis ordered.

Biryn paced impatiently. His nerves were more than frayed, his thoughts on Cylena and the horrors he could only imagine she must be dealing with. "What is taking them so long?"

Astiana was first to return. She walked up to Biryn, stopped his pacing, and placed her hand on his forehead. Instantly, the turmoil and anxiety disappeared. "Thank you, eh...I am still not sure what to call you. Grandmother?"

Astiana chuckled. "Gods, no. Astiana will do just fine."

Several servants arrived, carrying trays of food packs, wineskins, waterskins, and some fruit that could last more than a day.

Meanwhile, the others had returned. Opening their packs, they quickly gathered their supplies.

Astiana held out a small package. "What is this?"

"It's a skin suit. If temperatures are too cold, you wear it under your fleet uniform, and it will warm you," Aldis told her.

Erica snorted and reminded him, "What good will they do? The last time you had me wear one it almost fried me to a bacon crisp."

Biryn shook his head and looked at Laro. "Does she always utter such strangeness?" Then he asked Erica, "What is a bacon crisp?"

"Not sure how to explain. It is made from pork, meat from the pig. Long strips. Cooked, as in well done, like heavily smoked salted meat, and the strips are very crunchy."

"Erica, the skin suits have been redesigned. After our mission to find Icaras and the quest to the Cavaulal Mountains, our scientists redesigned the suit with a regulator to adjust the body temperature to a comfortable level. It will heat—or cool no more than is necessary for the wearer's bodily comfort," Aldis explained.

"Where are the weapons?" Biryn asked.

"Waiting for us in the hovercraft. Is everyone ready?"

They filed out of Biryn's quarters and headed for the courtyard to the waiting craft.

It didn't take them long to arrive at the Clyss. Biryn landed the hovercraft close to the pool. Before they left the craft, he handed each their weapons.

"Make sure your backpacks are all strapped on securely," Brenn said.

Biryn gazed at his surroundings. The Clyss was always full of life. The valley was carpeted in soft, green grasses, lush, colorful blooms surrounding the basin. Nyctea birds flew around them, chirping noisily, while fish jumped from the water of the pool and dove back in. How could everything be so peaceful here, while life elsewhere was in such turmoil?

Astiana placed her hand on his shoulder. "Biryn, you need to come with us."

She, Ciara, and Icaras, followed by Biryn, walked a short distance away from the others. They stood around Biryn, holding hands, and began to chant.

Dark clouds drifted over the Clyss, lightning slashing through them. A face appeared above the little group. Biryn gazed at it in awe. It was a kind face, lined, yet ageless, surrounded by long, snow-white hair. The god had a long, white beard. His piercing silver eyes gazed at them.

Small twinkling lights showered down, and Rania appeared, accompanied by Azphine.

"Who is it that called my name?" his voice thundered through the valley.

Rania and Azphine spoke in unison. "We did, oh, Sacred One."

"And who are the humans?"

"Sacred One, they are Ciara, dragon princess, Icaras, son of Cewrick, the evil sorcerer we defeated, and Astiana, the goddess recently released from her prison of stone. She was once Zohmes' mate. She has been granted permission to live as a human. The one standing in their midst is King Biryn. In infancy, Zohmes stripped him of his powers."

"And what is your request?"

"Sacred One, we request respectfully that you restore Biryn's powers so that we may rescue his lifemate from Zohmes' clutches. He has taken her to Yanata."

"There are several humans in the other group. They will not survive Yanata."

Biryn's heart sank. If the others could not survive Yanata, then the four of them would not stand a chance either.

"Sacred One, we —"

"Silence!"

Biryn watched the face disappear. "Now what?" he asked.

Ciara pursed her lips. "Ssh. The god has not left us. Just wait."

The face appeared again, white hair flying as if Izarus stood in a fierce wind. This time, they could see the upper half of his body. He was dressed in pure white-and-gold robes that fluttered around him. In his hand, his fingers encased in gold rings, he held a golden staff with a dragon's head at the top. He lifted the staff and shouted something in a language Biryn couldn't understand. The staff glowed and radiated a bright white light surrounding them all, not just the goddesses and the little group, but the others as well. Lightning began to strike down, touching each. Biryn had to close his eyes. The intense glare hurt too much.

The two goddesses chanted. He stood quietly waiting until a bolt of lightning struck him. Instantly, a charge circulated throughout his body. He felt warm all over. His skin tingled.

"The sacred council of gods and goddesses have agreed this is a special circumstance and with their approval, we have granted your request. Zohmes has angered us greatly. We will help you in your quest to rescue Cylena. We will also assist you in your missions to defeat Zohmes and send him to the bowels of Yanata for all eternity. Do remember, the evil that permeates Ierilia cannot be conquered and defeated overnight. You have all been granted limited magick, even the female from another planet. Go in peace, children."

The clouds faded. The god disappeared, as did the goddesses.

"Did I hear that right?" Erica said.

"I think so. It seems the god has gifted us all with some powers," Brenn answered.

"Wow. I don't feel any different right now. When the

lightning struck me, I experienced a shock throughout my body and was tingly all over, but now I'm back to normal." Erica rubbed her arms, her chest, then her legs.

Biryn walked toward them. "I don't notice a difference. I had the same experience, Erica."

Aldis shifted his pack on his shoulders. "I think we all did."

"Being able to shift into a lion is enough for me," Ivran added.

Ciara, Astiana, and Icaras joined them. "Time will tell what the gods have gifted everyone with. I know Biryn has his full powers restored, but we will have to guide him," Astiana said.

Erica scrunched up her face. "Well, if I have powers, I sure as hell need guidance."

"I think most of us will," Laro agreed.

CHAPTER TWO

Biryn's impatience was growing steadily. Cylena had been taken hours ago, and it could take days to rescue her. "Now we must go to Yanata. How? What do we do?"

"Everyone needs to stand in a circle, close your eyes, and join hands," Ciara told them. "The Sacred One will help us get to Yanata."

Frustration ate at Biryn. "And how will he do that? He is gone."

Ciara put her hands on her hips and gave him a pointed stare. "No. We just do not see him anymore."

Biryn grasped Astiana's hand. "Then let us do this. I have no wish to tarry any longer."

"We need to stay close together at all times. Under any circumstance, do not separate when we reach Yanata. I have no wish to lose any of you to the creatures below," Aldis warned.

"Yes, yes. We know this, Aldis. Please join hands and close your eyes as Ciara said we must." Biryn fidgeted impatiently.

They joined hands, forming a circle. Astiana looked at Biryn. "You must concentrate. Envision the doorway to Yanata. The spell we need will come naturally."

"And just how am I supposed to know what the doorway to Yanata looks like?" Biryn asked Astiana.

"Close your eyes. Concentrate. The vision will appear."

Biryn sighed and closed his eyes, surprised by the picture that formed slowly in his mind. A cave, dark and damp. Four tunnels led from it. The second one was illuminated by a white light. An inky black film covered the walls. Insects, the likes of which he had never seen, scurried about. Power burst through him, filling his body like water filling an empty vessel. Joining the chant that rose from Ciara, Astiana, and Icaras, he uttered words he did not understand. They seemed to come from deep within, appearing as if he had spoken the language all his life.

A fierce wind howled around them. Biryn could barely remain on his feet. Erica almost squeezed his hand off, her grip was so strong. The vision faded. He dared to open his eyes but only for a moment. The force of the wind increased. The sky blackened. A ring of electrical impulses touched them. Rumbling thunder sounded throughout the valley. His feet unwillingly lifted off the ground as he fought to retain his grip on the hard surface. Flight. He felt himself tunneling through a foggy void.

Silence.

He stood on solid ground again. The chanting had stopped. Biryn opened his eyes. They stood in the cave from his vision. The walls were black as if a fire had occurred within the cave. Strange insects crawled on them. The air smelled foul, almost like rotting flesh. Several sconces hung on the walls, torches lighting the interior dimly as if they were expected. The flickering flames sent eerie shadows and a soft glow throughout the cave.

"You can let go now," Ciara told them.

"One of those four tunnel entrances will lead us to Yanata,"

Astiana said.

"Yes, I understand the vision now. It is the second one from the left," Biryn told them.

"Are you sure, Biryn?" Brenn asked.

"I am very sure. In my vision, a white light illuminated that entrance."

"Glimmer sticks, everyone. They are in your backpacks," Aldis ordered.

Brenn approached the entrance and held his glimmer stick inside. "Single file. It is not wide enough for pairs. I will lead. Aldis, take up the rear."

Astiana activated her glimmer stick. "Be careful, all of you. Zohmes knows we are here. The four entrances are here to confuse us, separate us, so that we will split into different groups. Thank the gods Biryn was granted the vision for us to choose the right tunnel. Tread with caution. Danger lurks at every corner."

"Biryn, you will remain between Astiana and me," Ciara said.

"I will be behind Brenn." Icaras hurried to join Brenn.

They entered slowly. The tunnel was dark, the rotten stench even worse than in the cave. "Brenn, is this worse than the tunnels and caves you were in when you rescued Icaras?" Biryn called out.

"Yes, it is a hundred times worse. I doubt we will find beautiful crystal caves here and pristine water."

They walked for a long time without incident. Biryn occasionally had to brush away a slimy insect that had fallen from the ceiling, but they progressed nicely. "Astiana, how far is it to Yanata? Do you know?"

She turned her head slightly to answer him. "None, except Zohmes, have ever returned from Yanata to tell us. No. I do not know."

Ciara answered his question. "Rania told me it is very far. It will take several days."

Biryn's heart twisted. They still had several days before reaching Yanata? How many more after that before they found Cylena? She had to be frightened. By the gods, he should have been able to protect her from Zohmes. Should have sensed the sleeping spell. And Raollin. How could he have missed a change in the man? The putrid air closed around him. "It stinks here, and it is horrible, but I had expected a lot worse."

"Just wait, Biryn. We have only just begun our journey," Ciara told him.

Brenn stopped. "End of the tunnel. Cave up ahead," he called out.

They filed out of the tunnel and stood on a wide ledge. The cavern was huge, but a gaping chasm split it in two.

"Before we continue, we should eat and drink. It is well past lunchtime," Aldis said.

"Nowhere to sit," Erica commented. "I guess we stand to eat."

Biryn held his glimmer stick up. Sickly effluvium dripped from the cavern walls. On the other side of the chasm was another ledge, a number of tunnels leading from it. Bubbling pits of noxious, green matter pitted the ledge. Suppressing a shudder, he took his backpack off to take out some food and quietly ate it.

"How do we get to the other side?" Ivran asked after everyone had eaten.

"That is the easy part. I believe our journey is about to become a lot more interesting," Taylith said.

"Easy?" Erica queried.

Taylith shrugged. "Did you forget you are with two dragons? Ciara and I will carry you all over to the other side."

Astiana came to stand beside Biryn. "You need to concentrate again. We need to know which entrance to choose."

"Look, something just came out of the far tunnel and is now guarding the entrance," Laro pointed out.

"I do not trust what we see. Zohmes will mislead us. Biryn, close your eyes and visualize the map to Yanata," Astiana told him.

He closed his eyes and concentrated. Cylena's face kept interfering. She was foremost on his mind. Then her face faded, and he saw the tunnel entrances. Just like Astiana had predicted, it was not the far entrance they needed to choose. It was the one in the middle. Opening his eyes, he pointed at it. "That's the one. Not the one with the varmint guarding it."

It was as if the creature, or maybe Zohmes, had heard his words because it quickly moved to the entrance they had to take. Other creatures appeared out of the other entrances.

"The creatures are urglos. The vermin can be found all over Yanata. Zohmes must be in control of their hive," Taylith stated.

The urglos were covered in green skin, mottled with black-and-gray patches. The skin looked as tough as leather hide. They had rounded heads and snubbed faces with glowing red eyes on each side of their skulls. One opened its mouth, exposing two long fangs on both top and bottom jaws. The arms and legs were long and skinny with three webbed fingers and toes tipped with small, curving claws. Biryn had never seen anything like them, even in holographs. "I think we are about to face our first battle," he warned.

"What in the hell is wrong with Ierilia that you just can't have normal monsters like *Godzilla*. No, you have to have mutated alien miscreations with huge fucking teeth," Erica complained.

13

Biryn glanced at the Earth captain. Monsters could be normal? "I cannot even guess what this Godzilla is, but what is fucking?"

"Don't ask, Biryn. The answers tend to confuse one more than the phrases and words," Brenn informed him.

Aldis pulled his phaser out. "The proton phasers will reach the distance. We can kill the creatures before we fly across."

Biryn took his phaser and aimed at one of them. After watching his father die by the blade of his general, he'd had no wish to sit meekly on the sidelines while his guards protected him. Under Brenn and Aldis' tutelage, he had trained in all manner of weaponry used by his fleet and warriors.

They fired on the urglos blocking the tunnel openings, quickly disintegrating them.

Biryn scanned the entrances. No more urglos crawled through the crevices to stand guard. "This just seems too easy."

Brenn grabbed Biryn by the arm, pulling him away from the edge of the chasm. "We need to step back. Ciara and Taylith need room to shift."

Biryn watched Ciara and Taylith shift to their dragons, their scales glistening in the light of the glimmer sticks. He could not help but admire them. They were majestic creatures, Ciara a purplish-mauve, and Taylith a gleaming, sapphire blue. Ciara dipped her head and nudged Brenn in a quick caress. Then both dragons kneeled.

Brenn brushed Ciara's neck with his hand. "Ciara says they are ready."

Biryn, Astiana, Ivran, and Aldis climbed onto Taylith's back while Brenn, Icaras, Erica, and Laro climbed onto Ciara.

Biryn braced himself as Taylith flapped his wings, lifting above the cavern floor and following Ciara across the huge bottomless pit.

As soon as they were halfway across the chasm, more urglos poured from the tunnel entrances, their long legs allowing them to jump to great heights. They leaped into the air, attaching themselves to the ceiling of the cavern, and scurried toward the flying dragons.

Biryn fired his phaser at the creatures, killing several of them as they advanced. One leaped toward them and landed on Taylith's wing, hanging on by its claws. Biryn aimed his weapon at the urglo but hesitated to shoot. If he misfired, Taylith would be injured and unable to fly. The dragon turned his head and grabbed the urglo's leg with his jaw. Clamping his teeth around the appendage, he ripped the urglo from his wing. With a twist of his neck, he flung the creature across the cavern. It splattered against a wall, yellowish slime dripping down the wall in streams as the urglo slowly fell and rolled into the chasm.

Astiana gripped Biryn's arm. "You can lower your weapon now. I have shielded us from the aberrations and the heat of dragon fire. Ciara and Taylith will burn them to ash."

Biryn lowered his weapon. Ciara and Taylith flew side by side, incinerating the urglos and streaming fire into the tunnels until the onslaught ceased.

The dragons landed on the other side of the chasm. Biryn slid off Taylith's neck and joined the others near the cavern wall while Ciara and Taylith shifted back to their humans. Ciara grabbed Taylith's arm and began inspecting it.

Taylith shook his head at Ciara. "It is fine, Ciara. It healed when I shifted back."

"At all cost, avoid the bubbling green pits. The substance burns like acid," Astiana warned.

Biryn looked at one of the pits. The slimy substance was a bright, phosphorus green muck. Greenish plumes spiraled upward from it.

"Take another quick drink of your water, but sparingly. We need to conserve our supplies. Then get ready to move on," Aldis instructed. "This time I will take the lead, with Brenn bringing up the rear. Biryn, you must remain in between Ciara and Astiana. You are Zohmes' main target." Aldis pointed his glimmer stick into the tunnel to make sure no urglos remained.

They formed one line. Like the previous tunnel, it was barely wide enough for one man to pass through. The walls dripped with slimy sludge. Patches of red fungus grew from narrow recesses. A blob plopped on top of Biryn's head. He yelped and swiped at it. It was merely a blob of mucus.

Astiana turned swiftly. "Biryn, what is wrong?"

"Nothing. Slime dropped on my head."

Foul, ropy matter hung from the tunnel ceiling. Biryn heard the distant sound of wailing. "What is that?"

"Yanata is a place of torture and punishment and a place of filth that is beyond your imagination. When we arrive at Yanata's gates, we will face the monster that guards it. Rania has described it to me. It has a large round gelatinous body with eyes protruding all over its thick hide. Four reptile appendages extend from it, each with its own body and two heads. Each of those bodies has more extensions. There are many of them. It is called a vortextaur, and there is only one of its kind. It cannot be killed by any weapon or magick. It is there to stop the damned from attempting to escape Yanata. Each head has the ability to destroy by sending a lightning charge from its antennas," Ciara told them. "Rania has been feeding me a lot of information. We need to watch out for all manner of strange creatures. Wesmus, the ruler, is the fallen god of all evil and endings. He rules his filthy kingdom with cruelty, feeds the damned spoiled food, vermin, monster flesh, and tortures them for his pleasure. He lives in his luxurious castle. Well, if one can call it a castle. We will have to wait and see."

"How does Rania know all this if she has not been there?" Biryn asked.

"We do not question the goddess. I presume she was allowed to look into the book of knowledge," Astiana answered.

"All this reminds me of the stories of Hell we were told on Earth. If you murdered someone, or you were a really bad person, treated other people badly, led a life of crime, upon death you would end up in Hell. Is Yanata similar to that? I thought someone really bad was judged by the trial by fire and burned to ashes if they were guilty. I was told there is little or no crime on Ierilia," Erica questioned.

Ciara answered her. "As you know, we live for many centuries. Most will decide on their own that it is time to go to the realm of dreams. There are accidental deaths, of course, and the occasional murder. Murderers, traitors, and other heinous crimes committed by men or women, are judged by the trial by fire. As you know, if guilty, they do not survive and are incinerated. But their soul lives on and ends up in Yanata. And yes, there are those that do not lead an exemplary life. Their souls are judged by the gods and goddesses and sent either to the lower levels of the realm of dreams or to Yanata."

"I guess the realm of dreams is what we call Heaven on Earth. That there are levels, is interesting. Thanks, Ciara," Erica said.

"Stop!" Aldis shouted.

An enormous, scorpion-like creature blocked their path. Hundreds of smaller ones climbed the walls, and Biryn felt one near his legs. Drawing his weapon, he held the glimmer stick low and quickly incinerated the creature before it stung him.

Astiana called out to them. "Aldis, Erica, Ivran, Laro, think, concentrate hard, imagine yourself invincible, a shield around your body. Visualize it. Hurry, before the big one strikes. They are called snaps."

Aldis repeatedly fired upon the mother snap, but it kept advancing. The others fired at the smaller ones, killing one after the other, but there were hundreds of them.

"This calls for our intervention, Ciara," Icaras said loudly over their clicking sounds.

"There is not enough room to get close to each other. We have to meld our minds," Astiana said. "You, too, Biryn."

"Aldis, are you all right?" Brenn yelled from the rear.

"Yes. Because of the shield, the thing cannot touch me. We must have disturbed its nest."

Loud chanting echoed through the tunnel as Ciara, Astiana, Icaras, and Biryn's voices joined in a spell. The smaller snaps disappeared in puffs of fire and smoke, but the large one displayed its anguish and anger now even more. A stream of noxious gas poured from its gaping maw. Its claws groped for Aldis. He fired upon it again and again, now with the help of those behind him. They still couldn't kill it.

Somehow, it managed to reach through the protective shield, and they watched it grasp Aldis in a claw. It lifted him, ready to devour him, when the chanting became deafening. A lightning bolt struck the creature, and it dropped Aldis.

"Aldis?" Brenn shouted.

"I am fine. The shield still protected me."

"That was incredible!" Erica said.

The large snap crumpled to the ground. They had finally defeated it. Because of its size, they could not carry on, so Aldis disintegrated it with his phaser. "We can continue," he shouted.

Biryn carefully stepped over the carcasses on the ground, occasionally disintegrating one. He felt nauseated at the thought of his Cylena subjected to this place of utter horror.

They had walked for quite a while when they entered another large cavern. Like the other caves, the walls dripped with slime. Scattered throughout, were red bubbling pits, with fire dancing on the surface.

Brenn called out to them. "Stop. I think it is time for us to rest. According to my timepiece, it is late evening. We need to eat, drink, and sleep. One or two of us will have to watch over the others, but we will take turns. One of our magick users must be awake and alert at all times. I will take first watch with whoever is the least tired."

Astiana volunteered for first watch.

"And where do you propose we put our bedroll?" Erica asked, pointing at the filthy, slimy ground.

Icaras laughed. "Remember who you are with, Erica." He chanted, pointed at the stone beneath their feet, and miraculously, soft white sand appeared.

"Look, babe. The perfect romantic paradise honeymoon destination. The sandy beaches of hell," Erica told Laro.

Biryn felt bad for the newly joined couple. From the moment Erica and Laro had met, it had been one mission after another. And now they were with him on a trip in this foul place and remembering a ruined joining celebration. He would have to make it up to them.

"Okay. You guys have all this magic. You were able to transport us into this place. Why can't you just whisk us into Yanata? Wouldn't that be a lot easier?" Erica asked.

The others were already busy laying out their bedrolls, so she rushed to place her bedroll near Laro.

Astiana answered her. "Erica, you have been told many

times, we are only allowed to use our powers if permitted by the gods and goddesses. Though the gods and goddesses do not want Zohmes on the throne of Ierilia, I have come to believe this is another one of the tests for Biryn to prove his worthiness of the throne. Until our mission to the underwater sphere, he has never participated in any wars or missions. Therefore, we need to aid him on his quest to save Cylena and keep him safe."

They quickly ate some of the food, a piece of fruit, drank a bit of water, then crept into their bedrolls for the night.

CHAPTER THREE

Biryn woke with a start at the vision that haunted his dreams. Was it a dream or real? Had he really seen Cylena? He shuddered. In his dream, he'd seen her crouching in a corner. She was naked, dirty, and crying. He also saw a lot of other people. They looked human, but they were so thin, almost skeletal, and very pale. They huddled together in a group. All were naked. Something or someone had approached Cylena. "Eat," a loud, raspy voice ordered her. In revulsion, he saw a bowl of crawling insects shoved toward her. "If you do not eat, I will kill one of the other prisoners."

Astiana joined him. "Biryn, what is wrong?"

Taking a shaky breath, he told her of his vision of Cylena. "It was terrifying, Astiana. I cannot imagine my Cylena being subjected to such treatment."

"You have been given a vision that she is still alive. Be grateful for that." She squeezed his arm. "I wonder who the other prisoners could be?"

Ciara looked at him and frowned. "Maybe Zohmes has been capturing people for some time?"

Biryn *was* grateful to know Cylena was still alive, but the condition she was in, what she was being forced to consume for sustenance, was detestable. He would make Zohmes pay for every atrocity committed against her. Shaking off his anger, he focused his mind on the people that were imprisoned with her. "Those people had to have been there a long time. They looked very sickly, like they were starving."

Ciara shook her head. "I do not know. The goddess has not shared any information about the other prisoners."

"According to my timepiece, it is early morning. Eat, drink sparingly of your water ration, and we will continue," Brenn called out.

How could he possibly even think about food after the vision he had been shown? Biryn forced himself to eat some of the dried meat from his pack. He felt so helpless. He had been granted powers. *What powers?* So far, he hadn't been able to do anything but chant along with Ciara, Astiana, and Icaras, words that came to him naturally, though he had no clue what they meant. His frustration ate at him. To know he had been bestowed such abilities and not know what they were or how to use them made him feel incompetent.

Luckily, other than his vision, the night had passed by quietly. The shield Icaras had created around them had kept them safe. They had still taken turns sitting on watch, but it had hardly been necessary.

"Wait, before you remove the shield. Icaras, Astiana, what you told us about imagining a shield around our bodies, can we do that again if we need to?" Aldis asked.

"Yes, it is one of the powers granted to you by the gods, among a few other things."

"Like what?"

"We will find out in due time as the goddesses tell us," she answered.

Biryn scowled. By the gods, he was tired of the secrecy. Was this what his team had to deal with on each mission? It was a wonder they had managed to make it back to Cront in time with the ingredients for the veervaraine antidote. If not for Cylena holding him to the realm of the living, they would have been too late. Only the sword could kill him, he had been told. If it struck true. In this case, the sword had not struck true, but Zohmes had made sure to add the poison to the sword. Combined with the sword's piercing, it still could have been his ending.

"Time to pack up and go," Brenn shouted again. "Do not get close to any of the red bubbling pits."

"This is one humongous cavern," Erica commented as they carefully traversed around the red matter.

Biryn agreed. "Yes, it is big, though except for our mission to the underwater sphere, I have never been on any of your other quests, so I cannot compare. I am regretful now that I have never joined you on at least some of the others."

Astiana, walking beside him, patted him on the shoulder. "Biryn, the gods and goddesses have kept you safe all these years. It would have been unwise for you to participate in those missions. You were not ready."

"You said that this is a test of my ability to continue as ruler. Why did they not test me years ago?"

"I just told you why. It is also because you needed the others—your team—to assist you. Your team members had their own tests to complete before they were ready. That has now come to pass."

"Astiana, what I saw of Cylena in my vision was gruesome. How can we ever save her and the other captives?"

"Oh, ye of little faith. We will prevail. Wait and see."

Biryn wondered how Astiana could be so optimistic. Gods, he couldn't wipe the vision from his eyes. He knew, somehow, that Zohmes had bound her powers, ensuring she had no protection, no way to escape. For all her shy innocence, she had a core of steel. She would have escaped if she had the ability to do so. The memory of Cylena's voice whispered in his mind, *I fear being stuck back in the void I lived in for centuries… I fear losing you.* He refused to let that happen. She feared losing him. Instead, it was she who had been captured. He could not lose her.

Biryn's foot slipped, pulling him from his thoughts. He steadied himself and glanced around the cavern's wide expanse. It seemed like they had been walking forever. Finally, in front of them, there appeared to be an end to the cavern. It was nothing but a wall of rock, covered in oozing mucus and the bubbling red filth around which they had navigated. "And just how do you propose we continue if there are no doorways?"

Astiana stood beside him. "Nothing is ever as it appears."

"Search the cavern walls and floor for any kind of opening. There has to be a way out," Brenn said.

"There is no need to search. Biryn has the power within to find the doorway, just as he did the previous ones," Ciara said.

"Concentrate, Biryn. Just as you did before," Astiana told him.

Biryn closed his eyes. Clearing his mind, he focused on finding the way out of the cavern. A spot on the cavern floor lit with a bright light. He opened his eyes and pointed to one of the sludge-filled pools. "It is there."

"You've got to be fucking kidding me!" Erica exclaimed.

Biryn looked at Erica. "Really, Erica. What does this fucking mean? I have heard you use it several times already for all manner of things."

"Don't ask!" Ivran and Brenn shouted at the same time.

"If I am to listen to her strange words, then I would like to know their meaning."

Erica's face turned bright red under his perusal. "On Earth it is not a nice word, Biryn."

"And it means?"

Brenn, Ivran, and Aldis erupted in laughter. Biryn glared at them. "Quiet." He glanced at Laro. There was mirth in his eyes, and he was obviously trying to hold in his amusement. Of course, her lifemate would know. "Well?"

Laro looked at Erica and shrugged. "It is a word the Earth people use for mating, but Erica has explained that it can also be used in a bad way."

Biryn shook his head and chuckled. "We will discuss this later. We have to finish this mission quickly, Laro. If every other thought in Erica's mind is mating, you are in for serious trouble when you are finally alone."

Brenn shifted his pack onto his shoulders. "Now that that is settled, and you have expanded your knowledge of Earth language, we must continue."

Biryn looked at the doorway his vision had revealed. Unlike the other pits in the cavern floor, this one was filled with a black oozing substance. The surface bubbled and smoked. A putrid smell reached his nostrils. They would have to enter that?

Taylith approached the seeping matter and poked at the surface with his proton weapon. The black ooze dissipated, leaving behind an opening large enough for them to pass through, one at a time. "The black slime was nothing more than an illusion."

"I'll take the lead. Aldis, you take the rear," Brenn said.

Taylith stepped away from the opening when suddenly a large tentacle burst through, knocking him to the ground. The tentacle was a dark, sickly green and covered in thorn-like spikes. It whipped around and struck the floor, its spikes piercing the hard rock.

"Taylith! Shield yourself!" Astiana yelled.

Biryn pulled his weapon. But Taylith had managed to roll away from the dangerous spikes and shot at the tentacle. It exploded, showering the cavern with chunks of green mucous-covered gore. Several more tentacles erupted from the pools of slime. Weapons drawn, he and his team fired on the other tentacles until there was nothing left but clumps of putrid sludge.

Biryn slung some of the sticky substance off his pants and grimaced. "This is disgusting."

"Tell me about it. At least in the caves where we found Icaras we had water to wash the grime off," Erica said.

Clean water would be nice, but Biryn knew they would not be so lucky as to find a pool of it in these caves. He doubted their clothing would ever come clean again. The foulness of the caverns was probably embedded deep in the fibers.

"Let us continue. I will descend first," Brenn said.

Biryn peered down the opening in the cavern floor. Luckily it wasn't a long drop. They wouldn't need ropes to descend. They could jump in without an issue.

Brenn held his weapon and leaped off the ledge into the opening. He landed on the bottom, squarely on his feet, turning in a circle, making sure the area was clear. He glanced up at the group. "Ciara next."

Ciara jumped, then the rest of the team followed by Aldis, who descended last.

The tunnel was wider than the previous passageways. The walls were black and draped with a red mossy substance that seemed to pulse with movement, reminding Biryn of rivers of blood. The bones of strange creatures protruded from large patches of the red webbing.

"Do not touch the walls. The moss feeds on the unfortunate creatures that find themselves stuck in it," Astiana said.

The team continued forward in pairs, Biryn walking beside Astiana. "If this is a test of my ability to rule, why would the gods subject an innocent like Cylena to the horrors of this place?"

"Biryn, it is Zohmes' who has subjected Cylena to this madness, not the gods. We do not question the gods or why they allow certain things to happen. Do not anger them," Astiana admonished.

"I have ruled Ierilia for a long time. I believe myself to be a good and fair king," Biryn still grumbled.

Astiana stopped and turned to him. "Grandson, I am also the goddess of love and joy, now wearing a human skin. When Zohmes and I mated, it was a mating between love, joy, and goodness, and fire, hatred, and anger. Zohmes felt overwhelmed and angered by my attempts to temper him. He exiled me to the statue of stone and the bottom of the ocean after our son was born."

"What does that have to do with the gods testing my ruling of Ierilia?"

"I haven't been told, but this is my opinion. You are descended from love and hate. I think the gods are testing which will triumph under great duress."

Biryn felt anger well within. "That is crazy. I am here out of love for the woman who is destined to be my queen."

Ciara called out. "We must continue. Biryn, the gods hear and see everything, even our thoughts. Control your anger at them."

For the life of him, he could not imagine why Astiana would have mated with Zohmes. He forced those thoughts from his mind by thinking about his future queen. He continued on, avoiding the mossy substance on the walls and trying hard not to look at the skeletons embedded within it.

They came to the end of the tunnel. Below was yet another

huge cavern, but this one had a big, bubbling pool of water in its center. Water? Biryn shuddered. It was red. It looked almost like a pool of blood. Geysers sprang from it randomly. Large, insectoid creatures surrounded the pool, lounging on the edge as if enjoying a leisurely vacation on a beach. They were pale skinned, with hundreds of legs, bulbous heads, large ears, and a maw that could swallow a person in one bite.

There was no way to get down into the cave without the use of ropes or magick. And even then, how would they get around the swarm of giant insectoids?

"We cannot rest here for the night. There are too many of them," Brenn, turning around, said.

"What are we going to do?" Biryn asked.

"They will not harm us. They live on the substance that is in the pool," Astiana told them.

"Great, I get to spend the second night of my honeymoon cuddling with cute creatures from hell," Erica muttered.

"This is nothing, Erica. Wait until Zohmes sets his army upon us," Ciara answered.

An army? He frowned. Zohmes had been banished for centuries. How could it have been possible for him to amass troops during his captivity? Then again, Cewrick had lived for centuries. They did not know how long ago Zohmes had escaped Yanata and had partnered with the sorcerer.

Suddenly a long fish-like monster burst from the surface of the pool. In a flash, its wide flat head and gaping jaws snatched one of the creatures beside the pool and disappeared with it. The varmints scattered.

"I think we can descend into the cave now, but we need to be careful to stay away from the banks of that pond of whatever it is. The beasts feed on the fluid in the pool, and the monster below the surface feeds on them. It might like us, too, for a tasty dessert," Brenn warned.

One by one they slid down the rope Brenn had attached. When they all stood at the bottom, Brenn tugged and pulled the rope back in.

Ciara, Icaras, and Astiana walked to the far end of the cavern, which was now deserted. They created a small oasis for them to spend the night.

Biryn strode to the silvery sand. "I am so glad you are able to do this. Imagine sleeping here with all those things lurking around us."

"We have created a shield around our resting place. They cannot see us," Icaras told him.

They rested on the sand and dug in their backpacks for food. Erica screamed and jumped up.

"No fucking way am I eating this," she yelled.

That was their last supply of fresh food. After this meal, they had to survive on dried meat and water. Biryn took out what he thought was bread and smoked meat and dropped it. No wonder Erica had screamed. The meat was crawling with worm-like insects, and his bread was green and moldy.

"Go ahead and eat it. It is an illusion created by Zohmes," Ciara assured them.

"No way in hell am I eating any of that," Erica insisted.

Brenn took a bite of his bread. "It is fine. Believe Ciara. Enjoy the last of our regular food."

Biryn took a bite of his bread and found it was just like Ciara had said. It was an illusion. Then again, they were to survive on just dried meats and water? For how long? Tomorrow was going to be the third day. His mind dwelled on Cylena. Closing his eyes, he concentrated, and a vision appeared.

Huddled in a corner of her prison cave, she looked pale, and her body was covered in dirt and what looked like bruises. Anger welled within him. Was Zohmes abusing her?

A bowl of crawling insects stood next to her, another bowl filled with green liquid beside it. Zohmes was starving her, just like he starved the other humans he had in captivity. His heart bled, felt like it was shredded because he could not get to her right away. *I am coming, my love. We will be there soon.* Suddenly she looked up, straight at him.

No, Biryn, no. He wants you. He will kill you or keep you here. He wants your throne.

Was it even possible? *Can I communicate with her this way? Cylena, can you hear me?*

Yes, Biryn, I can hear you.

Is it safe to speak with you? We are all here, on our way to rescue you. Who are the other humans Zohmes holds captive?

Zohmes cannot hear me. I do not have my powers, but I do have control of my mind. I will not allow him into my mind. I do not know who the others are. They speak a language I do not understand. They are very ill, close to the realm of dreams.

I see that, my love. If you do not eat anything, you will become ill, too.

She gestured to the bowls on the ground near her. *I cannot eat the filth they give me.*

I understand. Cylena, you are my lifemate, my future queen. You need to survive. I do not know where we are or how far away we are from you, but we are following the gods' instructions. We will be there soon. Stay strong.

She lifted her chin defiantly. *I will survive no matter the cost, nor will I let him kill these people.*

Keep talking to me, sweet one. Sing me to sleep. I need to rest because the journey to Yanata is fraught with danger.

CHAPTER FOUR

Biryn woke, feeling completely rested. Cylena's sweet voice had sent him into a dreamless sleep. Was it all real? Had he imagined the conversation and her song?

"Astiana, is it possible for us to speak in each other's minds?" he asked.

"Yes, Biryn. Why?"

"Cylena spoke to me last night in my mind, but I was not sure if it was real."

Brenn sat down on the sand beside them. "What did she say?"

Biryn scowled. "Just that Zohmes wants me, either to kill me or keep me in Yanata. She does not know who the other captives are. She cannot understand their language."

"Did she say anything else?"

A vision of the sustenance provided to Cylena filled his mind. Disgusted, his stomach turned. "The food is revolting, so she is starving. It consists of crawling insects and foul water. I told her she must try and eat something and that we are on our way to rescue her."

"You can fix that, Biryn," Ciara informed him.

He cast her a surprised look. "What do you mean?"

"Contact her again. Concentrate hard, visualize her food,

31

then imagine turning it into something she might like, bread, meat. Turn her tainted water maybe into fruit juice."

"I can do that?"

She nodded. "Yes. You can do it for the other starving captives, too."

"I have such power, and you are just now telling me?" Frustrated, he shoved his hands through his hair. "I could have helped her sooner!"

Astiana gave him a consoling look. "We do not know what you have been gifted with until the goddess reveals your powers to us. You have a lot more magick than you realize. You will learn as you go."

"We cannot do it, but you are connected to her because she is your lifemate. Since her captivity, I have been unable to feel our bond. Help her, please," Icaras pleaded.

He placed his hand on Icaras' shoulder. He knew the pain the man felt. They both loved Cylena dearly. "You know I will, but how do I aid the other prisoners as well? I am not connected to them."

Icaras' pain-filled gaze held his. "Yes, you are, through Cylena. Her heart breaks for them I am sure, as mine would."

"Then I need some time to concentrate," Biryn said and moved to the far corner of the sand.

He closed his eyes and visualized her sweet face. *Cylena, love, can you hear me?*

Yes, Biryn, I hear you.

Help is coming. Now eat and drink. You have to.

I cannot. Look at what they gave me.

He saw her hold up two bowls, one with crawly creatures and the other with green water. He concentrated on the two bowls.

Oh, look, they gave me real food. There is even a piece of real bread, and there is clean water in the other bowl. How is that possible? I was sure it was the terrible living food they always bring.

Try and eat it as fast as you can. Each time they give you food, contact me?

You did this?

I will explain later. Can you show me the other prisoners and their food? I will help them, too.

A chill ran down Biryn's spine when he saw the prisoners through her eyes. They were alive, but barely. There were a lot of bowls containing living organisms, and a lot of bowls filled with various horrible liquids. He concentrated hard. Then he watched as they realized they had real food and water instead of the garbage they had been forced to try to eat. Like starving animals, they shoved at each other in their haste to get to the food. His heart bled for them. How long had they been there?

My love, we have to go now. This is day three, and I have no idea how much longer it will take to get to Yanata. Contact me when they bring you food again? We rest briefly for lunch. Then after the evening meal, we sleep.

I will. Thank you, Biryn.

I love you, Cylena. She didn't respond. Of course her mind would not be on their relationship, not under her present circumstances. But was he pushing her too fast, too soon? Then again, both of them had led such lonely, isolated lives for centuries. Now that he'd finally found his lifemate, all he could think about was them sharing their lives, making her his queen and rule Ierilia by his side.

Brenn's voice interrupted him. "We need to move on. Did you contact Cylena?"

"Yes. She is eating now, and so are the other prisoners."

"Good. We need to find out where we go from here. Biryn, we need you for that."

Biryn concentrated on finding the next doorway. It

33

appeared on the other side of the pool of blood. They would have to circle the bank of it to get to the opening. He gestured to the location. The wall was covered in the grisly moss and bones the same as the access tunnel. "It's over there. Beyond the water."

"We aren't supposed to touch the red stuff," Erica pointed out.

Biryn shrugged. "That is where the opening is. It will probably dissipate like the black ooze from yesterday."

"Let us continue," Brenn said as he took the lead.

Biryn followed again in the same order they had established at the beginning of the mission. It was frustrating the way Brenn and Aldis fussed over him. He wasn't inept. He could protect himself. He had made sure of it, but he understood why they did. They had become his family when he had no one else. He didn't want to lose them either.

Their path took them close to the edge of the blood pond. Biryn glanced at it. Unlike the night before, the surface was eerily still. Even the insectoids that had crowded the cavern were gone. He shifted nearer to the cave wall as they continued their progression past the pond. He had no wish to become fish food.

"The creature ate its fill. It is sleeping now," Astiana said.

"Sure, the huge piranha is sleeping. It's probably just waiting for one of us to step too close to the bank!" Erica exclaimed.

They stopped at the end of the cavern. Biryn scanned the wall but couldn't see an opening, just the red moss and bones. He stared at the lacework of veins in morbid fascination. The strange, pulsing movement he had noticed the day before grew stronger. The blood-like substance moved faster, causing the bones encased in the tendrils to twitch and stir. Decayed flesh and blood filled the empty cavities of the skulls. Strands of the moss shifted and grew, knitting limbs to torsos, torsos to skulls. Newly formed bodies lifted from the rock, creating a row of macabre creatures that blocked the exit that was hidden behind them. Hands grasped his shoulders, pulling him away from danger.

Aldis released Biryn. "I do not think these vile organisms are an illusion."

Biryn gasped as a vision filled his mind. He clearly saw Cylena, who was no longer huddled in the corner of the cave. Now she was chained naked to the wall. Blood caked her hair and skin. Lesions covered her body. Bruises disfigured her tear-stained face, and her eyes were swollen. The image cleared as suddenly as it had appeared. Booming, evil laughter echoed around him, rocking the walls of the cavern. A smoky mist, flames bursting through it, coalesced before him, taking the shape of a grotesque man. A mass of wild hair blazed like fire around his head. Hatred distorted his features. The figure ruptured into a mass of flaming black ooze, covering the creatures that guarded the doorway. Flames undulated across the grotesque entities as they surged forward.

"Zohmes," Biryn heard Astiana whisper beside him.

Rage pooled in Biryn's belly. Power he had never felt before coursed through his veins, infiltrating every cell in his body. *Gods, Cylena.* The image of her abuse fueled the violence of the magick swelling inside him. His gaze trained on the advancing monstrosities. His team surrounded him, desperately trying to fight off the attack. Magick blazed and weapons fired. The repulsive monsters, fueled by Zohmes' essence, staved off the team's defense. Biryn spied a tendril of moss snaking across the floor. It wrapped itself around Brenn's leg, yanking him off his feet.

A scream rent the air. Light flared from Ciara as she tried

to free Brenn by using her magick. The power within Biryn detonated. He held out his hands, ready to grasp the thing that had mangled Brenn's leg. Instead, streams of fire erupted from his fingers, pulverizing the twisting, snake-like vine. The monsters disintegrated from the force of his attack. The black substance, covered in flame, poured to the floor. The wispy smoke of Zohmes' essence coalesced above it, evaporating to nothingness.

Biryn staggered to his knees, reaching out with his mind to the woman who had captured his soul. The thought of her torture ripped his emotions to shreds. *Cylena, please, answer me.*

Biryn? You sound troubled. Are you all right?

Her beautiful form filled his mind. Her tear-stained face was unmarred. There were no chains, no sign of the mistreatment he had seen. *We ran into some unpleasant creatures, but my team and I bested them. I am uninjured. I just needed to see you.*

The vision faded. Biryn looked down at his hands. They appeared normal. Yet moments ago, fire had issued from his fingers. Was Cylena okay? Zohmes had given him visions, illusions. He had no idea what was real and what was not. He heard a soft groan. *Brenn!* He rushed to his friend and knelt beside him. The flesh on Brenn's leg had been shredded to the bone. It looked terrible. His stomach churned at the sight of the mangled flesh.

He watched Ciara step away from them. Why was she leaving Brenn? She could heal him. But he need not have worried. Ciara called out her dragon. Bending her long neck toward Brenn, she held her head close to the mutilated leg. Big dragon tears flowed. Instantly, the flesh sizzled, then began to pucker and regenerate. "Oh, to have such great magick," Biryn said softly.

"Step away from the wall," Icaras warned them. "I know what she and Taylith are going to do."

Biryn had not noticed that Taylith had also called out his dragon. They fell back as far as they could, supporting Brenn between them, giving the two dragons plenty of room.

They roared, their anger resonating throughout the cavern. Flames shot from their mouths, cleansing the walls of everything.

The two dragons flew throughout the cavern, eradicating every trace of the moss and oozing goo. They returned, and within seconds, Taylith and Ciara stood before them. Ciara hurried to Brenn.

"Are you all right, my warrior?"

"Yes, your tears have healed my leg. We can continue."

"I think we should rest," Aldis suggested.

"I agree," Ivran and Laro said.

Ciara nodded. "I think Taylith and I have cleared the cavern of all danger for now. Let us create a space to sit and eat."

Biryn quickly contacted Cylena again. *Cylena. Can you hear me?*

Yes.

Her voice sounded weak. *Have they brought you more food? We are about to have some lunch.*

Yes.

He saw the two bowls through her eyes and shivered, then concentrated. *I have changed it to edible food for you, my dear. Go ahead and eat it now. Look at the other prisoners. I will do the same for them again.*

How is this possible? How can you do this?

I will explain after we find you. Now eat. You sound weak.

They munched on dried, smoked meat and drank some water. While they ate, Biryn suddenly spotted a large opening in the wall at the end of the cavern. "The entrance is right there, behind us. It was there all along."

"It was hidden behind all that junk," Erica said.

"Junk?"

"That weird stuff."

Weird stuff? Biryn was beginning to understand why Brenn advised him not to ask Erica questions. He shook his head and turned his attention to Astiana. "Was that truly Zohmes we saw?"

"Yes, it was. It is difficult to believe he was once a very good-looking man. His hatred and evil ways have transformed him into the hideous, monstrous countenance he displays now."

Biryn screwed his face up in distaste. "How could you ever have joined with him?"

She raised her brow and gave him a pointed stare. "As I told you, he was a handsome man and very charming. There were two sides to him. The evil within his soul overpowered the good, and it consumed him."

Biryn shuddered at the thought that he was related to the gruesome face he had seen. He finally began to understand why the gods and goddesses were testing him. But he felt sure that such evil did not reside in his soul. He still didn't quite understand why they had waited for so long.

Astiana answered his unspoken question. "I do not know for sure, but these are our thoughts on it. It is because Zohmes desires the throne and your crown. Cewrick enabled Zohmes and weakened the spell that banished him. Cewrick wanted the throne for himself and made use of Zohmes. But if the team had not defeated Cewrick, Zohmes would have eventually. Cewrick was merely his tool, and because the sorcerer was corrupted by hate, it was easy for Zohmes to influence him. You helped rid Ierilia of the sorcerer, but it opened the doorway for Zohmes. So, it was time for the gods and goddesses to step in."

Brenn stood. "If we are finished, I would like to continue. My leg is healed, thanks to my mate."

"I like your sexy suit, Brenn," Erica told him.

"Sexy? What is that word?" Biryn asked.

"Sex is a word for mating. Sexy is seductive, provocative, maybe inviting. Geez, you're taking the whole meaning away from the word. I was merely pulling Brenn's chain, making fun of his torn suit showing off the leg."

"Pulling his chain? Erica, you have lost me."

"It means I was teasing him. Pulling his leg."

Biryn shook his head. "I did not see you pull his leg. Your Earth language is once again puzzling."

They got ready and headed for the far wall. Biryn could not believe how large the caverns all were. It took them quite a while to get there. Vermin scuttled out of their way. They had to move with caution because of the bubbling, slimy pits. At times the fumes were almost unbearable, so they had to put their masks on. Long, snake-like monstrosities slithered along the walls. Several times they raised their bulbous heads, their forked tongues reaching for the humans.

"I believe we have reached Yanata's entrance," Astiana said.

CHAPTER FIVE

The entrance led into a wide tunnel, spacious enough that they could all walk together. It wasn't that long. An orange haze glowed at the other end almost as if they were heading into Yanata's flaming underworld.

Loud wailing echoed through the tunnel.

"The voices of the damned," Ciara said.

The closer they approached the orange glow, the louder the wailing. It sent prickles down Biryn's spine. "Who are the damned? Were they not once human?"

"Yes, like I explained to Erica. For instance, you could find Lord Quadra there, who perished in his trial by fire. Many of the damned were once evil humans that centuries ago plundered and killed. The worst of them reside in the pit of fire. The rest serve Wesmus and are tortured without mercy. Yanata is spread over a great underground expanse, with tunnels going down to the various underworlds Wesmus has created," Astiana told them.

"Who is this Wesmus? Was he once a god, too?" Erica asked.

"Yes, he was a god who challenged Izarus. That did not go very well with the gods and goddesses. They cast him out and sentenced him to rule Yanata."

Erica grimaced. "Again, it reminds me of Earth's God. Lucifer or Satan — he is known by several names — was God's favorite, his anointed. He felt himself better than God and rebelled. With his army of rebel angels, he aimed to take over Heaven. God banished him to rule over Hell. Like your Yanata. It's interesting how this parallels with the Bible, a huge book that recorded what happened in those days. The big difference being, we only knew of one God, and His son, Jesus."

"What are angels?" Taylith asked.

Erica shrugged. "I've never seen any of course. They are always pictured as beautiful celestial beings with huge white wings."

"I would like to read this book you speak of."

"Taylith, remind me when we're back? I have a copy of it in my datapad."

They stopped when they got to the thick orange fog. "Behind this noxious gas we will face the vortextaur," Ciara said.

"How do we get through this wall of gas?" Biryn asked.

Icaras stepped to the front and peered through the tunnel opening. "That is the easy part. Between us, we can bespell it and create a safe path. What I am wondering is how do we get past the vortextaur?"

Biryn rubbed his chin. "If we can't kill it and magick will not work, surely there has to be another way? The gods would not have let us get this far if we could not get past it."

"The gods and goddesses will reveal the way. We will defeat the vortextaur in due time. First, we must bespell the fog and make our way to the entrance." Astiana held out her hands.

They clasped hands and chanted the spell, Biryn again concentrating on the magick and uttering the words that formed in his mind. A vortex took shape within the orange mist, modeling a pathway through the tunnel large enough for them to enter and move freely.

Biryn followed the team into the tunnel. The cloud swirled around the passage like a whirlwind. Ghostly apparitions flowed through it, each face a grotesque mask of pain. Gnarled fingers reached to pluck them from the path, only to stop short. The spell effectively protected them from the ghouls.

"Okay...that's freaking creepy," Erica said.

Biryn shook his head and laughed. He had no idea what she meant, but whatever it was, it seemed to fit the nightmarish spectacle of the spirit fog. "Freaking?"

"Yes! This is worse than Halloween!"

Should he bother to even ask? Biryn peered back at the disturbing display, revulsion pooling in his belly. The sooner they were out of the passageway, the better. A vision of Cylena pushed to the forefront of his mind, of the conditions she was forced live in and the food and drink Zohmes and his minions provided. Then of those poor people that were also caged. What he had faced so far paled in comparison.

"Look! Up ahead!" Brenn yelled.

Biryn glanced to the front. Thankfully, the end of the tunnel was in sight. He had heard stories of Yanata. All the Ierilians had. They were stories passed down through the generations, of a place so vile, only the most wicked and evil among them suffered such an unthinkable fate. Most of the people of Ierilia entered the realm of dreams upon their passing. To be sentenced to Yanata was the worst punishment imaginable or the greatest glory for the followers of Zohmes and Wesmus.

The group stopped at the exit of the passage. In the distance, Biryn saw an imposing entranceway — a rusty iron gate of immense proportions, flanked by a tall wall built of rocks. On top of the wall sat strange creatures. A blanket of smog obscured his view of what could be waiting for them near the doors. Directly in front of them, a walkway led to the gate. A pale paved road resembling polished bone gleamed in the light. Biryn shivered. Maybe it *was* bone. Pillars fashioned from piled rocks stood on each side. The bodies of Wesmus' prisoners hung from them in various stages of decay, their limbs still wriggling. Howls of agony cut through the silence. The cursed souls still lived. But of course they were still alive. They couldn't die. This was the ultimate torture. Even the skulls and skeletons they had seen appeared to still have life in them.

"Holy mother of God," Erica whispered.

The path to the gate was clear, their progress unhindered by ghouls or monsters. There was no need to protect the gates from intruders. Who in their right mind would enter Yanata willingly? Before long the rusty gates towered before them.

When will we get to Cylena? What else do we have to face in this place of horror? Biryn gazed at what awaited them beyond the gates. They weren't locked. But the horrible monstrosity guarding the castle entrance blocked anyone or anything attempting entry.

The gelatinous, almost transparent blob was as tall as the gates and much wider. Through its skin he saw its veins and organs. It was covered with protruding red eyeballs, from top to bottom and side to side. Many appendages projected from it, about the thickness of a man's leg. Each limb had its own head. Antennas protruded from each head. Each had a large, orange, glowing eye that glared at them. From each head, two more extremities grew. All the appendages moved steadily, keeping watch. Biryn realized they stood before vortextaur. "How do we get past that?"

"We know it can't be killed." Erica scratched her head.

Astiana ushered Biryn, Ciara, and Icaras close to them. "This is where we call on the gods."

Joining hands, they chanted, Biryn finding the words automatically. A fierce wind howled around them.

"Hang on to each other tight!" Brenn shouted.

The wind picked them up as if they were mere feathers. Within seconds, Biryn found himself standing on cracked steps facing battered old doors. The vortextaur had not seen them, and they were too far away now for the monster to stop them. From where they stood, Biryn saw how it defended the castle. A lone skeletal figure, once human, had managed to get over the wall. It attempted to run to the castle, but one of the long appendages saw it. Fiery bolts shot from its antennas, turning the ghoulish figure into a screeching, flaming statue.

Biryn shivered. "It is strange there are no guards here. How do we get inside?"

"Wesmus feels safe in his castle. The vortextaur will send anything that attempts to get close to it to Yanata's fiery pit." Ciara placed her hand on the rusty lock, then turned to look at them. "We will need the magick of the four swords to open it. You must touch the tips of the swords together as you did to free Astiana."

Taylith stepped forward and unsheathed his sword. "Gather around the door. Quickly."

Biryn, Erica, and Brenn pulled their swords. They stepped up to the doors, then stood beside Taylith.

Biryn held his sword forward so the tip would touch the other swords and the rusted lock barring their entry to the castle. Light flared from the blades as the engraved symbols began to glow brightly. The lock creaked and groaned, then fell to the steps beneath their feet. A blast of power radiated through Biryn's body straight through to the tip of the sword.

The heavy doors burst open, revealing a dimly lit room.

Brenn stealthily walked through the doorway first. "Nothing here. It looks deserted."

The women followed Brenn. Biryn waited until almost last. He slipped through the opening and noticed the doors were as thick as his thighs. Aldis was right behind him. Biryn's eyes grew accustomed to the dim interior only lit up by a scarce torch on the walls. The structure was old, decrepit, falling apart by the looks of it. Huge cracks ran along the walls and the ceiling. Giant cobwebs with huge spiders hung everywhere. The castle looked ready to collapse. Then again, this was Wesmus' domain. It had probably been here forever and would remain in Yanata infinitely.

"We need to find the entrance to the dungeons," Aldis said from behind.

"Biryn, close your eyes and concentrate," Astiana said while prodding his arm.

"It is too quiet. I do not see any guards or anything moving." Biryn closed his eyes and concentrated. "The entrance to the dungeons is at the end of this hall on the left."

"Wesmus does not think he needs guards. He believes nothing can get past the vortextaur. But we need to tread with caution because I am sure he has minions within the castle. He does not dwell here alone." Astiana resolutely stepped forward to head down the hallway.

Brenn hurried after her. "Astiana, wait. Let me go first."

Just as they got to almost the end of the hallway, a door opened, and two skeletal beings stepped out, spears ready when they spotted the group.

Biryn reacted. His weapon disintegrated them instantly. At least, that was what he thought. These creatures or fallen humans could not be killed, but they had disappeared under the onslaught of his weapon. "There is the door. Hurry."

With a mighty effort, the men managed to pull the door open. Biryn cringed at the sound of the creaky hinges that echoed throughout the vast hall.

A narrow stone stairway circled downward. They began to descend it as fast as they could. Biryn stumbled over a crack. He just managed to steady himself. "How far down is this? It seems as if we are going to the very center of the planet."

Ciara laughed softly. "You would not be able to withstand the heat, Biryn."

"I'm feeling a lot more than claustrophobic right now," Erica uttered.

Brenn snorted. "You and me both."

When they finally got to the bottom, there was no door. Simply an entrance to a large round open space. Biryn saw no guards. Large openings dotted the walls, covered with metal bars. They had arrived at the dungeons.

A soft moaning came from one of the caves. Brenn held up his glimmer stick. A sea of emaciated faces gazed at them. Thin arms reached through the bars. He quickly aimed his laser gun at the large padlock on the barred door. It clattered to the ground.

"Please. Help us," a weak voice said.

"Holy fuck. They speak English." Erica rushed to the dungeon and held up her glimmer stick.

"These are people from Earth! How the fuck did they get here?"

Biryn had followed her. "They are from one of your ships, Erica?"

Laro joined him. "They look close to death."

"If they came from one of the Earth ships, where is it and how did Erica's people get here?" Ivran wondered.

"Of course they're from one of our ships. Who else would speak English?" Erica snapped, showing her irritation at the dumb questions.

Biryn shone his glimmer stick at the other dungeons. They were all empty, except for the one they had just seen. Finally, he found Cylena huddled in a corner of the dungeon opposite one of the Earth people. "My love, we are here."

Cylena stood, desperately trying to hide her nakedness. Biryn called out to the women. "Does anyone have a spare suit in their backpack for Cylena and the other people?"

Erica rushed to them. "My spare skin suit will work to cover her. Unfortunately, we don't have enough for the others. There are thirty-two of them and only ten of us."

"We have bedrolls and some blankets. They can drape them around their bodies," Biryn suggested.

Erica nodded. "Some can barely walk. They are so undernourished it isn't funny. They must have been here since they crashed."

"They did not crash into Yanata. That would be impossible. Cewrick was still causing a lot of problems when your ship and the other ships crashed. Between him and Zohmes, I suspect they transported the crew down here."

Ciara and Icaras had joined them. They quickly demolished the lock. Cylena, now dressed in the skin suit, threw herself into Biryn's arms. His heart pounded so hard, he thought it would break his ribs. He held her close, silently thanking the gods and goddesses that they had found her, and kissed the top of her head.

She gazed up at him, her eyes filled with tears, her body trembling. "I knew you would find me." She clung to him for several seconds, then disengaged from his arms.

"We need to see to those poor souls. They are survivors from your planet, Erica?"

"Yes, Cylena, they are, but they can barely speak. They are too weak right now. I don't know how we are going to get them out of here."

Astiana glanced at Erica. "Now that Biryn has passed his first test, the gods and goddesses will help us return to the surface. All ten of us must form a circle around the people from Earth. You, too, Cylena. We will now call upon the gods and goddesses."

Biryn turned to Erica. "We did not bring our translators. You will need to explain to your people what is expected of them."

The thirty-two barely fit within the circle they formed. They huddled close together, holding tightly on to each other so they would fit within, the stronger ones supporting the very weak. Astiana, Ciara, Icaras, Biryn, and Cylena began to chant. A bright light appeared, so intense, they all had to close their eyes.

When Biryn dared open his eyes again, they stood in the valley of the Clyss.

CHAPTER SIX

The people from Earth were the crew of the Initiation Three. One of them, Jane Reed, the first officer, still lucid enough, had managed to give Erica that information.

As soon as they had arrived at the palace, Biryn had ordered them all to be taken directly to the hospital. Even with the food he had provided for them, it was too late. Many of the crew were too weak to eat and close to death. A full recovery would take some time.

The team sat around Biryn's food-laden table. All had bathed, wore clean clothing, and were glad to eat real food again.

Biryn and Cylena sat at the head of the table, holding hands. "Thank you all so much for helping to save me." Cylena held up her goblet.

They toasted to a successful mission, Cylena's rescue, and that of the survivors from the Initiation Three.

"We need to find their ship. The last thing we need is for Zohmes and Odoxon to get their sticky fingers on any of Earth's data," Erica commented.

"Rania informed me that the ship is on the ocean floor close to Garissa Island," Ciara told them.

"That's where Cewrick is," Laro reminded them.

Taylith sighed. "The gods have set an impregnable parameter around the island. How close to the shoreline is it?"

"I will speak with Rania again. It needs to be brought to land, or destroyed. We cannot let Zohmes get his hands on what is within the ship."

"We will discuss all this later. For now, I think everyone is anxious to go home to their loved ones. I, for one, would like to spend time with Cylena. And I think we all need to rest," Biryn suggested.

Even Icaras didn't argue and left for the rooms allotted to him in the palace.

Biryn stood and, taking Cylena's hand, pulled her up from her chair into his arms. Gods, she was so small and fragile. A vision of her in that cell pushed to the forefront of his mind. His body trembling, he hugged her tightly. How could he ever dispel the awful picture of her torture? "Gods, Cylena, you have no idea how thankful I am at this moment to hold you in my arms, to know that you are safe." He gazed down into her stormy gray eyes and caressed her jaw. "I am so sorry, my sweet. I failed to protect you from Zohmes."

Cylena covered his hand with hers, closing her eyes. She took a deep breath, then opened them, pinning him with an intent stare. "You are the one that found me, provided me with food and water...*rescued me*. How could you even think you failed to protect me?"

Biryn kissed her chin, her cheeks, then the tip of her pert little nose. "And you, my beautiful future queen, saved my life twice."

Cylena peered at him, a look of apprehension in her eyes. "Biryn, the gods and goddesses have decreed us to be lifemates. I know this. But you must give me time. It was not that long ago that I lived a lonely existence. I had no interaction with anyone except the people who raised me. You are a king, and I was raised a solitary farm girl. I spent my life on the outside of normal existence, alive but not truly living. Everything is new to me, so excitingly wonderful, yet also frightening. Especially now that Zohmes is bent on destroying you and your kingdom. Let us learn about each other first. Allow me to become accustomed to living in this world."

"Cylena, I realized when you were taken how deeply I have fallen in love with you. I can no longer imagine a life without you by my side. I will not rush you. I know what it is like to live an almost solitary life."

She stroked his hair, his cheek, her fingers resting on his lips. "Has your rulership been lonely?"

Biryn closed his eyes, savoring the feel of her fingertips brushing his skin. "Yes, my love. I have had no family since my parents entered the realm of dreams. I have only a few close friends." He opened his eyes and looked down at her beautiful face. "I have never permitted any wenches to warm my bed either." Tenderly, he tilted her chin and bent to place a kiss on her rosy lips. He felt them part and deepened the kiss. Clinging to her lips, he scooped her into his arms and carried her to his bed.

He lay her down and rested beside her, playing with a lock of her black hair. *Gods, I am behaving like a lovesick boy.* His stomach was in knots, and his heart thumped so hard it seemed as if it would burst from his chest. "I love you, Cylena."

"I love you, Biryn," she answered shyly.

He couldn't help himself. Those sweet words uttered from her lips fueled the fire in his blood. He gathered her into his arms and kissed her with all the passion pent up within him.

At first, she returned that passion, kissing him with a hunger that matched his own, until she suddenly pushed him away.

"No, Biryn. We cannot. We must not—"

"Do not worry, my love. That will wait until after our joining. You are safe with me." She relaxed, and he kissed her again.

They finally broke apart. "Let me ready myself for bed?"

"Of course, my love. I will do the same."

He watched her disappear into the bathroom and quickly divested himself of his clothing. After donning his nightclothes, he crawled back into bed and waited for her.

He was beginning to worry about her when she finally returned. Oh, but she was a beauty to behold. She wore a long, white nightgown, edged with lace at the scooped neckline and at the wrists and hem. Her hair hung in loose waves to her waist. Her gray eyes had a luminous glow to them. Her cheeks were flushed, and her lips parted. She approached the bed and climbed under the covers beside him.

Leaning on her elbow, Cylena gazed down at him, her eyes wide and innocent. "I don't care if it is unseemly. I feel safe when I am in your arms. And I need that now."

How could she possibly feel safe with him when it was his fault she had been abducted? He brushed her cheek with his hand. "But I didn't keep you safe, and I am so sorry for that."

She leaned down and tenderly kissed his lips. "You were not at fault, my king."

He took her into his arms and pulled her against him. His body ached for her, his cock throbbed, but he would never take her before she was ready. He took a deep breath to calm his craving. "Will you be my queen, Cylena?" he whispered near her ear.

She stroked his hair, twisting a lock of it around her fingers. "To be your queen will be a heavy burden. I love you, Biryn, but I must give this much thought. I am not sure that I am ready to be the queen that you need. Even if the gods and goddesses and the book of knowledge have decreed it, I am allowed a mind of my own."

"And if you go against them and the book of knowledge, then what happens? You would not be my lifemate if you were not my equal in all things," he whispered softly against her lips.

"My love, let us battle what is ahead first. All I can promise you now is that I will never leave your side."

He was relieved. That was all he could ask from her at this time. Gazing at her sweet face, he kissed her and held her tight. He could not worry now about their future. Her promise that she would never leave his side had calmed him. He heard her steady breathing and knew she slept. Closing his eyes, he tried to sleep, but rest did not come readily.

His thoughts plagued his mind and weighed heavy on his heart. Zohmes infiltrating the castle and whisking Cylena away. The death of his long-time friend and personal aide, Raollin. The storm that had destroyed a good part of Cront. What would Zohmes, in his fury, do next to usurp his rule? What atrocity would he plague the people of Ierilia with?

He felt Cylena shift in her sleep. Her head rested on his shoulder. Her hand was placed over his heart. The healing power she wielded so easily left her fingertips and sank deep into his soul, flowing through his veins and lulling him into a peaceful slumber.

Biryn peered out the window of his office in the throne room. It had been a long afternoon. The daily business of ruling a planet didn't stop, no matter the obstacles placed in his path. And his council could handle only so much of the day-to-day operations without him. More than fourteen days of peace and quiet. He could hardly believe it. His days had been busy with meetings, his nights—getting to know Cylena. Had Zohmes given up? Gods, he could only hope that were the case, but after centuries of Zohmes planning to take over Ierilia's rule, Biryn knew they couldn't be so lucky. The tests of his rule were not complete, but whatever the cause, the lull of Zohmes' torment, he was thankful for it.

Cylena's image filled his thoughts as he left his office. He envisioned her long black hair falling in unruly curls to her waist. He ached to feel the soft strands between his fingers. The way her stormy gray eyes shone with love—and passion—as she gazed upon him. He detoured to the palace treasury. His mother had once worn a necklace with stones that matched the gray of Cylena's eyes. It would look exquisite encircling her slender neck.

It had been centuries since he had ventured to the treasury. He had not gone there since his mother had entered the realm of dreams, and her belongings had been cataloged and placed within the vault. He punched the code into the security panel and stepped inside. So many memories were stored here. So much of it had long been forgotten. He had no wish to dwell on the remembered pain of losing his parents.

Biryn walked to the shelf containing his mother's jewels. His fingers lovingly brushed across the crown that she had worn. The crown had been passed down through the generations to each of Ierilia's queens. He grimaced. *Generations?* His family line was a fraud. He lifted his hand from the crown and picked up the box containing the necklace he sought. He opened the lid to ensure he was taking the correct one. Satisfied that it was, he closed the box and placed it in the pocket of his tunic.

He turned to leave when what looked like a frame covered in black velvet cloth caught his attention. Most of the portraits still hung on the walls throughout the castle. This had to have hung in his mother's chambers—a portrait that had been important to her. Curious of what lay beneath the cloth, he walked to it and gently pulled off the covering. Shocked, he gazed upon the painting. His mother sat on a blanket covering the grass in her personal gardens. Her face lit with happiness as she smiled up at another woman standing beside her. The woman could have been Cylena. They looked to be twins, except for the blonde hair and deep violet eyes. It had to be Cylena's mother. There was no other explanation.

Biryn grabbed the portrait and left the treasury, making his way quickly to the queen's chambers. As a surprise for Cylena, he had enlisted the staff to prepare the suite for her.

He opened the door to the chambers, removed the picture from the wall above the fireplace, and replaced it with the portrait he'd found. Happy with the results of his handiwork, he left the suite to search for her. Normally, when he finished with business for the day, he would find her with Icaras, spending the time he was away getting to know her brother and learning how to use her magick.

He knocked lightly on Icaras' door, anticipation filling him at the thought of sharing the evening with her. She had given him so much in the short time they had known each other. He couldn't wait to gift her with the necklace and the portrait of her mother.

Icaras opened the door, surprised. "What is it? Is Cylena all right?"

Biryn frowned. "She isn't with you? I just finished my duties for the day."

Icaras shook his head. "She left earlier to return to your

chambers. She had a lot of questions about our mother...and Cewrick. She seemed a little unsettled. I think our conversation upset her, but she told me she wanted to be alone to think."

"Thank you. I will talk to her. I know how hard it is to find out someone as evil as Cewrick is related to you."

Icaras grimaced. "It is just as hard growing up with that evil."

Biryn said goodbye and headed to his private chambers, hoping she was still there. If not, the palace was so huge, he'd have to enlist help to find her. He entered his rooms and noticed the sitting room was empty, but the doors to the balcony were open. Stepping outside, he found her leaning against the railing, gazing out at the gardens. "Cylena, is something wrong?" He took her hand and kissed each finger.

She turned to him. "I have been thinking a lot about you and I. Biryn, I am troubled about my birth parents. I know I can never meet my mother, but—"

"Oh, my love," he interrupted. "I almost forgot. I stopped by the royal treasury today." He took the beautifully carved, flat wooden box from the pocket of his tunic and handed it to her. "I would like to give you this."

Cylena took the box from him, a confused expression on her face. "A gift? It is not my birthday."

He gave her a lopsided grin. "Does it have to be your birthday to receive a gift? Open it."

Hesitantly, she opened the lid. Pulling her hand from his, she covered her mouth. An exquisite gold necklace lay on a bed of red silk. Gray crystals were embedded in the gold.

Biryn tenderly caressed her cheek. "The gems are the color of your eyes. Just like your beautiful eyes change according to your mood, the stones change color when wearing them against your skin."

"It is beautiful, Biryn. I do not know what to say."

"Nothing. Let me place it around your neck." He took the necklace from the box and draped it around her neck, fastening the clasp at the back.

Cylena held the necklace in place at her throat. "It is too beautiful to wear, Biryn."

"Nonsense. The treasury is filled with such beautiful jewelry, all of it meant for a queen. My queen."

He had finished securing the necklace around her neck and stepped back to gaze down at her. "See, look at that. Your eyes are a deep gray right now because you are troubled, and the stones are the same color."

"Thank you, my king." She stood on her toes and kissed him fleetingly on the lips.

"My king? Now tell me what troubles you. You began to say you know you can never meet your mother. But that is the other surprise I have for you. Come with me to your new chambers." Taking her hand, he pulled her inside and to the doors adjoining the queen's chambers to his.

"I already told you, I do not need my own rooms. A man and woman that love each other share the same bed, the same quarters." She sounded flustered.

Biryn gave her hand a gentle squeeze. Depending on the circumstances, he often burned the candle at both ends. The rulership of Ierilia came at a certain cost. Mainly his personal time. "My love, I often have meetings in my quarters. At such time you may want to retire to your own private domain. At night, you will always be by my side. Of course, that is if you have decided—"

Cylena interrupted him. "I have not yet decided. That is what is troubling me—my birth parents." She looked disturbed as she continued. "Hirsuta, my mother, was a loving, sweet, and caring woman. Icaras has told me so much

57

that my head spins, but what he has told me about Cewrick plagues me more than anything. Cewrick was my father. Why would the gods want you to join with his child? What if the same evil that consumed him resides in my soul? Why would they have decreed that I become your queen? Zohmes was banished to Yanata. Yet he now reigns terror upon us. What if somehow Cewrick is freed?"

"Cylena, the gods have banished him to Garissa Island from which there is no escape. You need not fear."

"You do not understand. I do not fear him, but I fear him for *your* sake."

Hoping to dispel some of what bothered her, Biryn pulled her further into the room. "I am almost forgetting the surprise I have for you. Look at the wall above the fireplace."

Both hands flew to her face. "Oooh! That is a painting of my mother, of Hirsuta with another woman. Maybe they were friends? I look like her. You found this in the treasury?"

"My mother and yours must have been close once. Yes, it was in the treasury, well wrapped in a dark cloth, with some of my mother's belongings."

"She is beautiful, Biryn. Thank you, thank you, thank you! You have brought my mother to life for me. I will treasure this gift more than anything." Tears trickled down her cheeks.

Placing his arm around her waist, he pulled her against him and stroked her hair with his free hand. "I love you, Cylena. I will do anything for you."

"Biryn, if I tell you something, I am afraid you will think badly of me."

"Never."

"Is it strange, even though I know Cewrick was an evil man capable of terrible deeds, that I have the wish deep within me to meet him? To know my father?"

Shocked, he stepped away from her. "My love, you do not

mean that."

Reaching out to him, she placed her hand on his chest. "Your heart beats faster. I have made you angry."

"No, not angry. Shocked, but never angry."

"Deep within, I wish I could know both my birth parents. You at least have given me the gift of my mother's image, but yes, I would like to gaze upon the man who killed her, who sent Icaras to the bowels of Ierilia and threw me into the river. His blood flows through my veins, and therefore I can never join with you."

"Cylena, you are so alike to your mother. You are all love, sweetness, joy, happiness, and kindness. Just look at her portrait."

"But knowing Cewrick is alive, the wish is there to meet him."

"I hope the gods do not honor your wish, and I pray the book of knowledge has no such words written in it. I am sorry, my love, it is a wish that can never be realized."

Cylena straightened her shoulders and gave him a pointed stare. "It can. And until such time as I face the man who could destroy so much, whose hatred is said to have conquered any goodness within him, I cannot be your queen."

Biryn's heart splintered. She couldn't possibly mean what she was saying. No one was allowed on Garissa Island. What she asked for was not possible. "Cylena, be reasonable. Cewrick tried to kill you at birth, among the other atrocities he performed throughout the centuries. The gods will not allow you to visit him, nor will they allow him to go free."

Cylena stroked his cheek. "I care deeply for you, Biryn, but how can I make you understand? I feel him inside me just like I felt Icaras. Gods, I feel his anguish. His soul is tortured. How could he possibly be the evil being he is said to be if all I feel is the pain of a broken man? How can I possibly be your queen if I feel sympathy for the man who destroyed so much?"

Biryn pulled her into his arms, holding her close to his chest. "You see goodness in everything you touch." He kissed the top of her head. "Let us save this conversation for later. I invited Brenn and the others for dinner. It has been days since we have seen them. But I also asked your adoptive parents to join us. You haven't seen them since the night you were abducted. I thought to surprise you. Dunmore should be arriving with them shortly."

Cylena stepped back and looked up at him, her eyes filled with happiness. "Thank you for that. I have missed my parents greatly." She stood on her tiptoes and kissed him. "Let me freshen up. I will be back shortly."

Biryn watched her retreating back. The fact that she wished to see Cewrick puzzled him, but her sympathy for the man disturbed him. He knew this had to be another test, but what could possibly be the correct solution? Defy the gods and grant her wish or protect his kingdom at all costs? Deep down he knew he would forsake his kingdom if she so wished. He also knew this was one wish he could not make reality for her. No human could set foot on Garissa Island except the unfortunate ones banished to live there.

Cylena gazed at her reflection in the mirror over the sink. Her face was so like her mother's that they could have been twins, except for the raven hair and gray eyes she had inherited from her father. Gods, she could feel how much Biryn loved her. It welled within her, pulsing along their connection, and she loved him, too, fiercely. The past fourteen days had been joyous. She had spent the mornings and afternoons with Icaras, learning to control the raging storm of magick within her.

Her evenings she'd spent with Biryn, getting to know the man the gods and goddesses had chosen as her lifemate and learning what life was like to finally be free. Yes, she was Biryn's match in more ways than one, but how could she possibly risk his crown if Cewrick was the evil man everyone knew him to be? She closed her eyes, clutching her chest, and took a deep, shuddering breath. The anguish that gnawed at her along her father's connection was so crippling at times, she didn't think she could bear it. She had to find out the truth of the man, who Cewrick really was, before she would ever complete a joining with Biryn. She would not allow the crown to fall to a child of Cewrick's blood if the man was truly evil.

But if she could not join with him, what would happen to the crown? Biryn's subjects expected him to give them a queen, a woman chosen by the gods and goddesses, and more importantly, an heir. He had waited decades for his lifemate. And it was written by the gods that the king wed a lifemate, not just any woman.

Cylena felt torn in so many directions. The brother she was slowly getting to know, the knowledge that she was Biryn's lifemate, an evil twisted father, and her desire to do right by everyone.

She had resigned herself to living a life of solitude on the farm, of never falling in love, never having friends. Then suddenly, her whole life had been turned upside down. In so many ways she was happy to now lead a normal existence, to be like others. Biryn filled her heart with joy, their love a tangible thing that continued to grow, quenching a thirst her parched soul had hungered for centuries to fulfill. But to agree to complete their bond and become Biryn's queen? Not until she learned the truth. She shook the turmoil from her mind and concentrated on freshening up.

CHAPTER SEVEN

Biryn sat at the table in his private chambers and looked at his guests. Family. That is what it felt like. It had been so long since he'd had a family. He usually took his meals in his rooms alone. Brenn would join him at times, but this was different. Cylena sat by his side, bubbling with happiness. She made his life complete. Her parents had left earlier. Dining with the king made them uneasy, so after they'd eaten and said they were tired, he had Dunmore take them back to Icaras' castle.

Cylena grasped Biryn's hand under the table and turned to gaze at him. "Thank you for inviting my parents, Biryn."

Biryn smiled. "They can visit you anytime you wish, my love."

He turned as Aldis walked up to him carrying a tray filled with small glasses and a bottle of eldalas spirit. Aldis set the tray on the table and poured the fiery liquid into each glass. Biryn took one for himself and Cylena.

After each member of the group took a glass, Aldis seated himself at the table and held his glass up. "May all of our evenings be this quiet."

Biryn took a healthy drink from his glass and set it on the table. *Quiet? The lull before a storm maybe*, he thought.

It was as if Erica had heard his thought. "No one else finds it weird? The quiet? There is no way in hell Zohmes has given up."

Biryn fidgeted with his glass. "No, he hasn't given up, but a thought occurred to me. When he possessed those creatures in Yanata, he was wounded. He had to be. Do you think he had to take this time to heal?"

"I don't think he was wounded, but it is possible his power was weakened. He would need time to rest after possessing a human and the monsters we fought," Astiana stated.

"Or he could be planning something much worse," Ivran said.

Biryn picked his glass up from the table and focused on the people he called family. "Let us enjoy tonight. Zohmes can intrude on our happiness another day." He lifted his glass to take a sip of his drink when he felt ripples of movement beneath his feet. The table shook hard enough to lift it from the floor.

"I knew he couldn't leave us the hell alone! He must have been listening to us!" Erica yelled.

Biryn dropped his glass on the table and stood, pulling Cylena to her feet with him. A flash of light drew his attention to the open doors of his balcony. He rushed through the doors, followed closely by the others. His hands clutched the railing as he gazed out at Cront. The city looked fine, but tremors still shook the palace. Erica stood next to him. Her hand suddenly grasped his arm, her other pointing at what rose from the ground. Shocked, he looked at the mountain rising slowly.

"Biryn, Brenn, what in blazes is going on? I can't believe my eyes. It's a mountain forming right before our eyes. It's a fucking volcano!"

He glanced at her shocked face. "I have never heard of this.

Neither have I ever seen a mountain suddenly appear from the ground." He stared at the unnatural phenomena. Plumes of smoke spiraled up from the summit. Balls of fire spit from it, raining down upon the landscape below, setting shrubbery and trees ablaze. The mountain continued to rise until it towered over the city of Cront, the surrounding landscape lit up by the fiery balls in an eerie glow.

"Look, there are traders on the road on their way home from market," Cylena shouted.

"We need to send out rescue teams. I will see to it immediately." Aldis abruptly turned and walked back inside.

Biryn's heart sank. *Quiet? Peace?* This was Zohmes and his accomplice at work. "Zohmes' doing."

"Erica, you have experienced this on Earth?" Brenn asked.

"Yes. We have volcanoes on Earth. Many of them are inactive, but sometimes there is an eruption. Thing is, they already exist. This mountain rose magically from the ground."

Biryn scratched his chin. "There are no such mountains on Ierilia. What do we need to prepare for?"

"Lava comes from deep down. It is made up of crystals, volcanic glass, and bubbles. When it reaches the surface, it cools and turns into a glowing mass of slush. It will run from the mouth of the volcano, the crater, and down the mountain, instantly killing and destroying anything it touches, turning humans into charred statues. On Earth, lava buried whole towns."

"So we should issue an evacuation order?"

"It looks that way. The palace is a good distance away, but Cront is not."

Astiana interrupted. "We need to step in. Ciara, only the gods can assist us. We cannot change the landscape and neither can the goddesses. Come with me. We need to seek help."

A steady rain of white ash flakes began to drift down, covering the gardens below.

"I've never seen a live volcano except in movies," Erica told them. "I pity the poor traders that were on their way home."

Biryn wiped perspiration from his brow. "It is getting much warmer. Brenn, check on Aldis and see if rescue teams have been sent out."

"Oh my God! I don't fucking believe it. How is that even possible?" Erica yelled.

He turned back to look at the mountain. Amidst the smoke and fireballs, the nose of a spaceship appeared. It ascended slowly as if pushed from below. "What is that?"

"It's another one of our ships!"

"Your ship? From Earth? How can it come from below?" Biryn wondered.

"You question that, Biryn? Tell me, how the hell did the crew from one of our ships end up in Yanata?"

"Zohmes."

"Exactly. What puzzles me is this ship looks intact — at least from what I can see of it from here. And it's ascending on its own now. Look, it's leveling out and getting ready to land. That means there is someone at the controls."

"I do not see the lava you described," Laro commented.

"No. This is not a regular volcano. It appears Zohmes has again tried to copy one of Earth's natural disasters but didn't succeed completely."

As sudden as the mountain had appeared and begun spewing smoke and fireballs, it sank back into the ground leaving the ship hovering above, then landing. Biryn heaved a sigh of relief. "The gods and goddesses have helped to restore the landscape to its former state."

He had no sooner spoken when Astiana, Icaras, Ciara, and

Cylena returned. They walked out onto the verandah, Cylena joining him. She leaned against his side. "The gods and goddesses assisted us. But they also issued a warning. We need to beware of the people aboard the ship. Zohmes and Odoxon have infiltrated their minds."

"As if the rescue of one crew isn't enough to deal with." Erica looked at Biryn. "I will need to go to that ship and take some of my own crew with me. Like right now, before they make contact with anyone."

"Aldis, can you arrange this? You need Brenn, Aldis, Laro, and Ivran to accompany you. I do not think we should involve any of your crew, but you cannot go alone," Biryn told her.

"Why not?"

"You heard what Cylena said. Zohmes and Odoxon have poisoned their minds somehow. They may not be the same people you knew on Earth."

Ciara agreed with him. "They may not even remember where they are from. Icaras, Astiana, and I need to go, too."

Biryn sighed. "If everyone is going, then we shall all go. Aldis, have you received recent reports on rescue efforts?"

"Our crafts and rescue teams were on the scene very fast. I am sad to report there was a loss of life. Five traders. Quite a few of the marketers were badly burned and are in the hospital. Many of our people are beginning to panic. Too much has happened of late. The dragons and urcals, the stone statues, the black funnels, the hurricane, and now this."

Astiana stood and motioned to Ciara, Icaras, and Cylena. "Come, before we leave, we need to speak to the gods and goddesses. The people of Ierilia need their help."

The flight to where the ship had landed didn't take long. Erica shook her head to clear her troubled mind. She'd not even had the chance to visit the survivors from the Initiation Three. And now there was another crew to deal with. One part of her was happy that another of their ships had crashed on Ierilia. But after Cylena's warning, she wondered what she was up against. That left one missing ship. Was it asking too much to hope that the last ship was somewhere on Ierilia and its crew had survived? "Damn, maybe Zohmes has that one in his sticky fingers, too," she muttered aloud.

"What did you say, love?" Laro asked, squeezing her hand.

"I was thinking about the last missing ship."

"And Zohmes. I heard you say his name."

"Yes. Who knows if that bastard has the last ship, too."

The hovercraft landed not too far from the ship. Erica gazed at it as she stood at the bottom of the steps. "It's the Initiation One. That leaves only the Initiation Four that is missing."

The ship sat quietly. Its engines had been turned off. There appeared to be no activity, no open door, yet someone had landed the spaceship. And if the ship was intact, surely the crew had seen the hovercraft's approach?

"Wait here. I can open the door."

"Erica, you are not to go alone. Who knows who or what is inside. Aldis and Brenn, go with her," Biryn commanded.

They were halfway to the ship when the heavy metal door slid open, and the automatic steps descended. Erica looked up at the figure standing at the top. She knew him well. It was Daniel Moore, captain of the ship. He was a tall, handsome black man. She recalled he had been very popular with the ladies. His usual broad smile was missing. He looked stern, forbidding almost. "Daniel! It's me, Erica!"

"Stop right there!" Daniel ordered while walking down the

steps, followed by his crew.

Erica saw at a glance that all thirty-two had survived and appeared to be well. "Daniel, it's me. Erica Martinez."

"They warned me this would happen. You are not who you say you are."

"Who warned you?"

"The dudes that saved us. Show your true self. Same goes for the rest of you. If you can even understand what I'm saying."

"Obviously I can understand you or we wouldn't be talking. Holster your weapon. No one here means you any harm."

Daniel laughed sarcastically and smirked at her. "Then why are you all carrying weapons?"

"We didn't know what to expect. The ship looks completely intact. How is that even possible after plummeting to this planet? You all look well. Where did you crash? Where have you been all this time?" She noticed confusion among the crew.

"I don't know where we crashed. The dudes that brought us out of stasis told us it wasn't safe to leave the ship and to remain inside until now."

"Who were the dudes? And if you were told not to leave the ship, how did they get in and out?"

"Stop it with the questions already. Show yourselves, reveal who you truly are. I was told the creatures here can change their appearance at will and not to believe anything I see or hear."

"Wow. Talk about brainwashing. And these dudes spoke English? Where are they now? Can we talk to them?"

One of the crew appeared from behind Daniel. "Erica, if that is really you, you'll know what happened in the bar we went to after the dinner, the night before we left Earth."

"Jenny! I'm so happy to see you. Of course I know. You were drunk out of your mind and began to do a striptease on top of the table."

"They're also mind readers. She can hear our thoughts," Daniel said.

"Damn, Dan. I wasn't even thinking about that particular incident. Something else happened that only Erica knows about."

Frustration gnawed at her. How could she prove to them that it was truly her? She turned to Ciara. "Can you do anything?"

"Keep talking to them."

Behind her, Erica heard Ciara, Icaras, Cylena, and Astiana chant softly. They stopped.

"We cannot break the spell that caused them to believe everything they were told," Icaras told her.

"Cuff them and bring them inside," Daniel ordered his crew.

Aldis, Brenn, Ivran, and Laro instantly took their fleet weapons out of the holsters and pointed them at the Earth crew.

"No weapons needed. This I can stop." Icaras lifted both hands.

The crewmembers that advanced toward them slowly, their weapons trained on them, hit a wall.

"You would attempt to capture your own kind?" Erica yelled.

"Shoot!" Daniel commanded.

They fired their weapons, but the lasers didn't penetrate Icaras' shield.

"How many dudes, as you call them, were there?" Erica asked.

"Three."

"What did they look like? And did they have names? Daniel, everything is not as it seems. How can I prove to you that it's me? Of course we could fetch the rest of my crew. And the others from the other ships. Would that convince you?"

"Ours is the only ship that crashed here."

"Sorry. There were five more ships that crashed. Not everyone survived."

Daniel's crew began to shift uneasily and murmur to each other. "I think it is really Erica," Jen told him loud enough for her to hear.

"It's about time you returned my hairdryer, Jenny," Erica said.

"See! I told you!" Jenny began to run toward them, but Icaras' shield stopped her.

"Let her through, Icaras. Can you do that?" Erica asked.

In a flash, Jenny stood beside her. Erica hugged the now crying young woman. "See, it is really me, Jen. There is nothing to be afraid of. You've all been brainwashed by whoever managed to take you out of stasis."

Jenny stepped back. Erica held her by the shoulders. "Introductions can come later. Now, can you tell us the names of the dudes?"

Wiping the tears off her flushed cheeks, she told them. "Weird names. One of them is a very old man with a beard almost to his toes. His name is Odoxon. Then there is a wild-looking guy, Zohmes. And the third one's name is Cewrick. He never says much."

"Oh my God! Cewrick? He's escaped?" Erica looked at her companions, saw the shock written on their faces, especially Icaras and Cylena's.

"Escaped from where? But they saved us," Jenny said.

"Honey, Cewrick is a badass sorcerer and so is Odoxon.

71

Zohmes is a fallen god. Between the three of them, they are mighty powerful. I'm glad they didn't erase your memories, but they tried to brainwash you into believing that I am not who I really am and that what you see is not what it seems. And these people that are with me honestly saved and helped us all. They are truly real. There is nothing fake about any of us."

Erica glanced over to where Daniel and his crew were, but they had gone back inside the ship, and the door was closed.

"I believe you." Jenny's blonde ponytail bobbed as she nodded vehemently.

Erica gazed into her earnest green eyes that were still suspiciously moist, Jenny obviously trying to control her emotions.

"How many of our people made it?"

"A hundred and sixty-two. There is still one ship missing. The Initiation Four. You have no clue where you crashed or where you've been all this time?"

"Nope. How are we going to convince Daniel? I think many of the crew are inclined to believe you. But he's being a stubborn ass."

"How about you go with us, and we'll try and fill you in on what's all happened since our arrival here. Then you can go back and talk to them. Think that's a good plan?" Erica looked at Jenny, then at the rest of the team.

Biryn agreed. "I think that's a good idea, Erica. Brenn's estate is closest."

Erica acknowledged this suggestion. "Yes, I think it will help if she talks to Mark and Laura."

"We can't leave their ship unguarded. We don't know what else Zohmes may have planned," Brenn said, drawing Biryn's attention. "I will assign Trevain and a small unit of warriors to guard the ship while we discuss this." He grabbed his communicator and contacted Trevain.

"What good is guarding the ship going to do? If Daniel decides to take off and land it elsewhere, what can you do? Shoot it down?"

"You're right, Erica. No, we don't want to shoot it down unless it poses a threat to Ierilia. But I think we do need to keep a discreet watch on it. We cannot allow these Earth people to leave the ship and go into Cront. Not at this point. After we talk to Jenny, we will see if she can reason with the captain."

"For added security, I will place a shield around the ship," Icaras told them. "It will stop any attempt to take off."

CHAPTER EIGHT

Biryn sat beside Cylena at the table in Brenn's kitchen. Her hand felt like a vice around his fingers as Jenny finished explaining the rescue of her ship. He glanced at Cylena. All color had drained from her face, her attention on Icaras.

"Zohmes, Odoxon, and Cewrick rescued us. They never told us where they found the ship or where we crashed. They brought us out of stasis and kept us safe. I don't understand why they would lie to us about you. I know Daniel is convinced that they speak the truth and only want to help." Jenny finished her recount of the Initiation One's rescue.

"How could Cewrick have possibly escaped from Garissa Island?" Laura asked vehemently.

"I am not sure how, but Zohmes and Odoxon must have found a way to break the bonds that held Cewrick to Garissa," Astiana said.

Laura began to say something, then clamped her lips together.

"It's okay. Laura, tell Jenny what happened to you and Mark," Erica encouraged her.

"Cewrick used black dragons and giant birds to capture me and Mark! He tortured us, then later had those creatures drop us into the forest to feed his monsters." Laura continued to tell her tale of the kidnapping and agony at Cewrick's hands.

Biryn's stomach turned as Laura described what had been done to them. He noticed that her voice no longer trembled when she said Cewrick's name and fear no longer darkened her eyes. She had come a long way from the anguished young woman he had first met at Brenn's betrothal party.

He gazed at Taylith standing behind her, his hand resting on her shoulder, his body going rigid at her mention of the black dragons and their part in Cewrick's atrocities. Did Laura realize that Taylith had belonged to Cewrick for centuries? That he could have been the one that delivered her to Cewrick? The curse had forced so many into slavery to the sorcerer.

Biryn turned to Cylena. To hear the tales from victims other than her brother had to alarm her. Tremors shook her body. Tears spilled down her cheeks. The guilt she felt slammed him so hard he could barely breathe. He caressed her cheek, drawing her attention. "You are not your father," he whispered.

"If that madman has escaped, then I want to be part of the mission to capture him," Mark growled after Laura had finished speaking.

Biryn had seen the holographs and footage from the missions, of Laura and Mark when they were at death's door. Talking wouldn't convince the captain of the Earth ship, but maybe the visual proof would. "The footage and holographs from your missions, can they be transmitted to the Earth ship?"

"I don't see why they couldn't except they don't have holographic technology. We have managed to transfer the data from the other ships to our databases," Aldis stated.

"The holographs are pretty graphic, and most of the

information is classified. Are you sure you wish to share them with a group of people subject to Zohmes' whim?" Brenn asked, frowning.

Biryn tapped his fingers on the table. "I don't think talking to the captain will convince him, but the images we have of Laura and Mark, of finding Icaras, of the hurricane and the Earth people we rescued from Yanata, surely will. Just to name some. We have recordings of every single mission. Visual proof of the evil Zohmes, Cewrick, and Odoxon, are capable of, will show a truth much more convincing than words."

"I have all of that information on my datapad." Aldis drew Biryn's attention. "We don't need to transmit the data if Jenny is willing to return to the ship and show her people the images. Trying to transmit the information to them would take too long and, if they have no holographic capability, be sort of useless."

"Transfer the pertinent information to a clean datapad. I have no wish to give them more information than necessary to convince them of the truth."

Erica interrupted. "We can't send Jenny back in there without protection! What if they turn on her?"

"She will have protection." Biryn handed Jenny his communicator. "Before you enter the ship, touch this button to turn it on. We will hear everything that occurs. If your crew tries to harm you, we will hear it and can help you."

Jenny took the communicator from him. "This is all very overwhelming. My mind is still trying to process everything you told me. Thank you. I will make sure to turn it on. I feel like I am in some kind of dream."

"I can imagine. I ask myself every day if I am still living in a dream world," Erica said.

Jenny fidgeted with her ponytail, twisting it around her

fingers. "I suppose we need to go back to the ship soon, so I can talk to Daniel and the crew."

"Yes. Sooner is better. Aldis, has the information been transferred to the datapad? I believe we are ready to return to the ship."

Aldis handed Biryn the datapad Brenn had fetched for him. "The images and footage are transferred. Is Jenny ready?"

Jenny nodded. "I am. But it is a task I'm sure as fucking hell not looking forward to." She fingered the translator Aldis had attached to her uniform.

Biryn chuckled. "We now have another person using Erica's strange expressions."

"What does he mean?" Jenny whispered to Erica loud enough for Biryn to hear.

Erica giggled. "They've had a lot of fun with our strange words from Earth."

"I'm awed that I am sitting at a table with royalty and yet you are so at ease, Erica."

"It takes a bit of getting used to. Biryn is cool."

"You call him by his first name?" Jenny asked.

Biryn smiled at Jenny, then raised his eyebrows at Erica. "Cool? I am not cold, Erica. Jenny, doesn't your family call you by your first name? These people have become the family I never had. That includes Erica. She has become an invaluable member of my team, and I have become quite fond of her. Let us get back to your ship. I would like to resolve this before nightfall."

Biryn stood and held his hand out to Cylena, helping her from her seat. He sensed the torment she felt, and it nearly broke him. All he wanted was to handle the situation at hand, then return to the palace and comfort her. He followed the others to the hovercraft, ushering Cylena up the steps and to her seat. He sat down beside her and strapped in.

It didn't take long to reach the Earth ship. Aldis landed the hovercraft in the same area as earlier. Biryn followed the others outside, Cylena standing close to him. He grasped her hand and gently squeezed.

Biryn turned to Jenny. "Remember to turn on the communicator so we can hear you. Everyone is wearing translators, so we will all understand what is being said. If you are in danger, we will step in."

Erica patted Jenny's shoulder. "Everything will be fine. They will listen to you when they see the proof."

Jenny walked to the door of the ship and turned on the communicator. She looked back at them. "Can you hear me?"

Erica spoke through her device. "We can, Jenny. You can go inside."

Biryn watched as Jenny punched the code sequence into the console by the door. It slid open, and she entered the ship.

"Where is Daniel?" Jenny's voice came through loud and clear.

"You're back? They didn't hurt you? He is on the bridge. I will walk with you," a man said.

"No, they didn't hurt me at all. But the guys that saved us? They are devils! I have to talk to Daniel," Jenny said.

They heard footsteps, then the sound of another door sliding open. The murmurs in the background indicated the whole crew was on the bridge.

"I know you brought them back with you, Jenny. I won't let those aliens take over the ship." Daniel sounded irritated.

"Daniel, what Zohmes told us? It's all lies. That *is our* Erica. I also met with and talked to Mark and Laura. What Erica said is true. Those people helped them."

"They have you brainwashed. Remember what we were told. They can change themselves into anything or anyone. Well, you can join them. Leave the ship. Now! I won't have you putting everyone in danger," Daniel argued.

"If you think about it, it doesn't make sense. How could they even know what Erica, Laura, and Mark look like? Zohmes and Odoxon also told us that ours was the only ship that crashed on this planet. So try and sort that out in your fucked up brain. And if you still don't believe me, then believe *this*!" Jenny said.

"What the hell is this? They have such advanced technology? Oh my God! Is that really Mark and Laura? And that's the crew of the Initiation Three in some kind of dungeon. They look like they're at death's door." Daniel sounded shocked.

Screams erupted. The sound of Zohmes and Odoxon's booming laughter filled the air around Biryn. "We need to go in now!" he yelled.

Erica ran in front of Biryn and the rest of the crew and punched in the code, opening the door to the ship. "Follow me. I think they are on the bridge."

Biryn grasped Cylena's hand as they raced behind the others to get to Jenny and the rest of the Earth crew. Chanting echoed through the corridors. It had to be Odoxon. The voice didn't sound like Cewrick's.

They reached the bridge of the ship. Biryn pulled Cylena inside. The whole crew, including Jenny, writhed on the floor as if in pain. Three robed figures stood over them. One of them turned and looked at Biryn, his hideous countenance filled with hatred. *Zohmes*. No sooner had he pinned him with his stare, when he disappeared, along with the other robed man who had to be Odoxon.

The third man stood frozen in place. He pulled his hood from his head, revealing his face. The old man Biryn remembered was now young, his once gray straggly hair now dark as a raven's wing. His storm-gray eyes swirled with power, his gaze riveted on Icaras, then on the woman by Biryn's side. An expression of shock contorted his features.

Cylena's hand crushed his fingers. Biryn tried to shift her behind him. She wouldn't budge. From the corner of his eye, he saw Icaras move to stand in front of his sister.

Cewrick clenched his jaw. His hand reached out toward Icaras and Cylena. "My...my...children. You must go to Niqine. Zohmes wants the book of knowledge. She must be protected. He can never get his hands on the book." Cewrick grabbed his head with both hands and screamed. Black smoke and flames curled around him, his body fading into a swirling vortex.

They were stunned at what they had just witnessed. Biryn shook his head. Was this the same Cewrick who had reigned terror on Ierilia for so long? Was Cylena right about him?

Icaras, Cylena, Astiana, and Ciara had joined hands and chanted a spell. The crew stopped writhing and slowly stood upright. Daniel was the first to speak.

"I can't believe the pain they just inflicted upon us. I have never been in such agony. My deepest apologies. It seems we were all duped. Me more than any of my crew."

Biryn stepped toward him and held out his hand. "Greetings. I am King Biryn, ruler of this planet."

"A king?" one of the women uttered. "Wow."

One by one they introduced themselves until Brenn interceded.

"We can continue this conversation at my estate. Please come with us to our hovercraft."

"What about the ship?" Daniel asked as they left it. He turned around to gaze at the Initiation One. "Oh my God! How could we even fly? I'm sure I heard the engines."

They all stood on the grass now, looking at the badly damaged ship. Biryn nodded. "It was an illusion created by

Odoxon. Now that the spells have been lifted, the ship appears in its true state."

"But the console, the controls, everything was functional," Daniel said.

"Again, illusions. In your mind everything was operating normally. That's what they wanted you to believe. It was their magick that caused the ship to move and land. We will have it transported to our space engineering department. Aldis, will you take care of that?"

"What about our personal belongings?" Carol, the first officer, asked.

"Everything will be gathered, tested for contaminants, packed, and then returned to you," Aldis answered. "Now we must go."

CHAPTER NINE

When they arrived at Brenn's estate, Gieth had prepared enough food to feed an army. It never ceased to amaze Biryn how Brenn's chief cook was able to produce such large meals in record time.

"I can't remember if I've ever eaten such fantastic food," Daniel commented while rubbing his stomach. "Even our goodbye dinner doesn't equal to this."

"Now that you have all had time to relax and have eaten and had your fill, we will transport you to the compound," Biryn told the Earth crew.

"Don't worry, Daniel. That's what they call it, but it's like a hotel. It's where all of us from Earth have stayed until we learned their language and studied their history. Quite a few of ours are already working and living on their own. Some of the crew from the Initiation Three are still in the hospital, but from what I've learned, all are healing. You'll be among friends." Erica helped herself to some more of Gieth's delicious cake.

"There are still so many unanswered questions," Daniel complained.

Erica set her fork on her plate. "I understand, but we are all safe and there is plenty of time in the future. Several of my crew have been assigned as liaisons and are available to answer any questions you most certainly have."

"The hovercraft is here to transport you to the compound," Aldis announced.

After the Earth crew had left, Brenn's staff filled several glasses with eldalas spirit and set them on the table. Biryn reached for one and pushed it into Cylena's hands. She looked shell-shocked and pale, and her body trembled, but the power that was hidden within her simmered beneath the surface, her eyes glowing with the strength of it. "Drink this. It will help calm you."

Cylena took a sip from the glass, wrinkled her nose, then handed it back to Biryn. "Thank you, but this is a little too strong for me."

"How could they have released Cewrick from Garissa Island? No one can set foot there. The gods bound him!" Icaras stated in an agitated tone.

"Zohmes and Odoxon, obviously. But what does that matter now? Cewrick is free and now the other two are after the book of knowledge," Ivran said.

Biryn caressed Cylena's hand and turned his attention to the people seated around him. The events of the day were shocking for all of them. They had so much to discuss, but some of it could wait. The book of knowledge had been coveted by Cewrick for centuries, and he had never gotten his hands on it. It was safe. But why had Cewrick issued the warning? He himself had wanted the book. Now he did not want Odoxon and Zohmes to have it? Jealousy? He still coveted the book for his own use? He replayed the scene in his mind when Cewrick had set eyes on his son and daughter, the expression on Cewrick's face as he had gazed upon them — shock, then a glimmer of happiness and hope. Really? Had Cewrick's short time on Garissa Island changed the man? Made him see his evil deeds? A thought suddenly occurred to him. Zohmes was capable of possessing anyone and anything. What if he had possessed Cewrick centuries ago? What if all of Cewrick's evil was none of his own doing? He shook his head to clear the thoughts.

Cylena needed him now, and he would attend to her. "It has been a very long and stressful night, and the suns will be rising soon. We will return to the palace for what is left of the night." Biryn gestured to Cylena, Icaras, and Astiana. "We will continue this discussion in my chambers after we have all had a few hours of sleep."

"I could use a few hours of sleep." Aldis tried to stifle a yawn.

It didn't take them long to reach the palace after they said their goodbyes to the team. Once the hovercraft landed, Biryn ushered Cylena to his private quarters while Icaras and Astiana made their way to their own rooms.

Biryn opened the door to his chambers and led Cylena inside. He pulled her close and brushed his fingers down her cheek. "You look drained, my love. We should retire now for the remainder of the night."

She gave him a wan smile. "You have no idea how exhausted I am. Yes, I want to go to bed."

"Then to bed we will go." Placing an arm around her waist, he guided her to his bedroom.

She placed a quick kiss on his jaw. "Allow me to freshen up?"

"Of course."

He waited impatiently. All he wanted was to hold her. Yes, his hunger for her was a steady ache, almost too much to bear at times, but he would honor her wish and the promise he'd made. They would not be together until their joining. The sound of running water reached his ears, and all he could think about was her skin, wet from her bath, glistening in the soft light of the moons. Before she came to his bed, he quickly took his erection in his hand and moved the skin back and forth. He'd done this so many times over the years. It wouldn't hurt to do it a while longer. Picturing her beautiful face, her eyes, her pert breasts peeking through strands of her wet hair, he managed to release his urgent desire. Though deep within, he still wanted nothing more than to be one with her and complete their lifemate bond. Pain twisted his insides. Her refusal to be his queen was a rejection of that bond. He closed his eyes and prayed to the gods that they would be able to resolve the issue about her father and her misgivings about their joining.

"Biryn, are you asleep?"

Startled, he opened his eyes. She stood beside the bed in a snow-white night dress edged with white handmade lace. He was glad she made use of the wardrobe he'd had his seamstress make for her. Her gray eyes gazed down at him. He saw the love reflecting from them. "Yes. I was waiting for you, my queen."

Cylena crawled into bed beside him and nestled against his chest. "I am not your queen. Please do not call me that?"

He toyed with a strand of her damp hair. "My love. Is that better?"

"Yes. Much better." She sat up, resting on her arm, and looked down at him, chewing her lip. "My king, Cewrick...my father is foremost on my mind."

Biryn wrapped the strand of her hair he was toying with around his finger. "You do not want me to call you my queen, so please stop calling me your king?"

"I am sorry." She leaned down, placing a featherlight kiss on his lips, then looked at him pleadingly. "I need to talk about my father. I cannot get him out of my mind. While I bathed, I had a vision. Odoxon and Zohmes have Cewrick in captivity."

His eyes widened in surprise. Dropping the strand of hair, he cupped her chin and studied her face. "Are you sure it was a vision? It could have been Zohmes playing tricks with your mind. He used a terrible vision of you to torment me before we rescued you from Yanata."

She shook her head. "It wasn't Zohmes. Rania blessed me with the vision. Cewrick's warning to us was against Zohmes and Odoxon's wishes. They imprisoned him and are punishing him in a terrible manner. Between them, they have bound his powers so he cannot defend himself."

"My love, do not ever forget what your father has done. His deeds were just as nefarious."

She closed her eyes, a pained look crossed her features, tears spilling down her cheeks. "The vision *showed* me the facts. The man he was wasn't my father! Zohmes took possession of him shortly before my mother gave birth to us. Just like he did to Raollin and John from Erica's crew. Cewrick learned the truth of it all while he was bound on Garissa Island. Everything Cewrick has done—every horrific misdeed—was Zohmes' doing while he inhabited my father's body."

Biryn gently wiped the tears from her face. "Cylena, do you realize what you are telling me? What this could possibly mean?"

She grasped his hand and held it to her cheek. "Yes. I do. It means that my father is innocent of everything that happened during his reign of terror. Including what was done to me...to Icaras. He didn't kill my mother. Zohmes killed her."

He knew before asking what she would want of him. Was it truly a vision from Rania that Cylena had been shown? When they had encountered Cewrick on the Earth ship, he hadn't seemed to be the same vicious man he'd been before his defeat and imprisonment. "And what do you wish to do now that you were given this vision?"

She released his hand, her eyes engaging his, that storm of power within her causing them to glow softly in the darkened room. "I want to rescue my father."

Biryn clenched his jaw. Of course she would want to rescue Cewrick, and fool that he was, he would help her to do so even if the gods punished him for it. "My love, I would do anything for you. I am willing to die for you...even give up the throne if you required me to do so. What you are asking is against the gods and goddesses' decree."

"But I received the vision from Rania. Why would she show me this if we are not supposed to act upon it? If you will not help me, I will go alone." She pulled the covers from her body and attempted to rise.

He clasped his arms around her and pulled her back to the mattress. "First, we need to get some sleep. It has been a long night, and I know you are tired. We will talk again in the morning when we both have clear minds."

Tears spilled from her eyes as she regarded him. "Don't you understand? We need to go *now*. I *have* to save my father."

Biryn took a deep breath and released it. Her pain ripped at his soul, but rescuing Cewrick from Odoxon's castle needed careful thought. "Gods, Cylena, do you realize what you are asking me to do?"

She wiped the tears from her eyes. "Yes. While I was getting ready for bed, I gave it much thought. You have a flyer. We can leave before the suns rise for Odoxon's castle. That's where my father is held. Zohmes is there, too."

"So we just fly to that castle and rescue him... Just like that? My love, this needs careful planning. I need to contact the team." He turned to take his communication device off the bedside table.

She pulled his sleeve to stop him from using it. "No. Do not call them. You and I can do it."

He let her take the communicator from his hand. "Cylena, this is beyond madness."

She placed the communicator on the table by the bed, then gave him a pleading look. "I *have* to do this. I love you, Biryn, but I can never join with you until I have all the answers I need."

Biryn grimaced and held his forehead. This situation was going downhill fast. "And how do you propose we go about this?"

Her hand brushed his shoulder. "We fly to the mountain where Odoxon's castle is. We infiltrate it. Between the two of us, we have enough magick to counter anything that would stop us."

Powers? He didn't have a clue what those powers consisted of, much less how to use them. The castle was a fortress, surrounded by huge, thick walls. The entrance of tall iron gates was more than probably guarded. Besides getting through the gates, there were sure to be guards at the castle doors. Okay, if they managed to overpower those, and got inside, they would be sitting ducks if they were caught in Odoxon's castle. "My restored powers are new to me. I do not know how to use them yet. Astiana and Ciara have promised to teach me, but there has been no time. And now you're talking as if it is as easy as that?"

Biryn felt his resolve weakening. Cupping her chin in his hand, he tilted her head and tenderly kissed her. Gods, he loved her so much and would do anything she asked, grant her every wish. "We will get dressed and stealthily leave the palace. I will help you, my love…even if your wish is against my better judgement."

Her face lit with expectation. "I will dress quickly." She slipped from the bed and hurried to his dressing room.

Biryn heaved a sigh, but seeing the hope written all over her face and in her eyes, he squashed his misgivings. He quickly gathered his clothing and dressed. Lastly, he strapped the scabbard on and placed his sword in it. It was the only defense he had, that and the powers he still did not know how to use, and Cylena's magick that she was still learning. He wished he had a fleet weapon, a proton phaser, but Aldis always collected those from them after a mission.

After Cylena joined him, he opened the door. The two guards posted outside his doors began to follow them. Biryn turned and held up his hand. "We wish to walk alone and enjoy a glass of wine and a snack in the privacy of my gardens. Remain here." He thought it a plausible explanation for their backpacks and hoped the guards believed him.

"Sire, we—"

"Silence. Resume your positions."

They calmly walked to the palace doors, waited for the guard to open them, and leisurely walked down the steps as if they were going for a midnight stroll. As soon as the heavy doors closed, they quickened their pace to head for the gardens, then the landing pad located just behind the beds of flowers.

Biryn landed the flyer at the base of the mountain just as the suns began to rise. "It has been a long time since I have piloted one of these. I suppose one does not forget."

"Now what?" Cylena questioned.

"We need to climb up the mountain to the castle. I still think this is a bad plan. There is dense forest on this mountain. Predators could be hiding anywhere, and we do not know what kind of protection Odoxon has around his castle. But I will do anything for you, my love. Even give my life."

"Biryn, the gods and goddesses will protect us."

He helped strap her backpack on, his thoughts still on the utter recklessness of this venture. She had been sheltered and wasn't used to the rigorous demands of a mission such as this. They had very few supplies with them. He'd grabbed a waterskin for each and a wineskin and some leftover cheese and bread from the evening meal. It would not last long.

She adjusted the straps of her backpack on her shoulders. "Thank you."

He could not help but admire her bravery as she resolutely began up the slope toward the forest. Hurrying to catch up to her, he took her hand in his. "Stay by my side, love. Pray to the gods we do not encounter morcougs."

She shivered. "I have seen these beasts on your holographs. They are fearsome."

"Yes, and not easily defeated, if ever."

Odoxon's castle had been built high on the summit and was surrounded by thick stone walls. He had seen pictures of it. It had sat empty all this time while Odoxon was in banishment. He could imagine the state of decay it was in now. Unless his minions had remained there to take care of the place. Would they have waited for centuries for the sorcerer to return? He shrugged. Anything was possible.

The forest was so dense that the suns' rays could not penetrate the thick foliage. Small animals scurried as they climbed. Birds scattered.

"We've been climbing for a long time, and it seems quite peaceful," Cylena remarked.

"Yes. I hope it remains so."

He'd no sooner spoken when the loud crackling of branches sounded. Biryn pulled her to stand behind him. He drew his sword and wished for a fleet weapon.

Unfortunately, they had all given them back to Aldis. Not that a fleet gun would do much good from what Brenn had told him. Two morcougs appeared in front of them. "Run! Hide!" he yelled at Cylena and pushed her toward the trees.

Remembering his training and what Brenn had told him, he gazed at the giant creatures. The throat. He had to get to their necks somehow. *Stay away from their drool. Their claws.* One of those beasts had almost killed Brenn with one swipe from its claw.

For now, the morcougs stood still and just watched him. Biryn didn't dare move. One movement and they would attack. He hoped Cylena had found cover. But his hope was in vain. Behind him he heard her soft chant. She was trying to bespell the beasts.

"Cylena, run for your life. Your spell is not working," he hissed through nearly closed lips.

The sound was enough to antagonize one of them. It advanced and swiped at Biryn. He jumped fast enough to evade the large claw. The other morcoug joined in the fight. Biryn tried to envision the shield around him and Cylena, but it didn't work. What good did his magick do if he didn't know how to use it? He lurched back as another claw lashed out and barely missed him. He struck at a claw, but the blade of his sword bounced off the hard, scaly skin.

"Where are the gods and goddesses now?" Biryn shouted, seeing Cylena flee into the forest from the corner of his eyes, the second morcoug hot in pursuit of her.

Oh yea of little faith.

Had he really heard that whisper in his mind? A rushing of wings, a stream of fire, and both morcougs lay writhing on the ground. More fire, and they were soon mere piles of ashes.

Biryn's heart stopped trying to pound out of his chest. He scanned the dense brush and trees, looking for any trace of

91

Cylena. "Cylena? Love, where are you?" he called.

"I'm here." She rushed into his arms.

Ciara and Taylith calmly walked up to them. "What were you trying to accomplish, Biryn?" Taylith sounded angry just before he called out his dragon again.

"Cylena had a vision from the gods, and —"

Ciara's glare bore into him. Her violet eyes flashed with contained fury. "And you didn't think you needed to inform the team? If we had not arrived, do you really know what would have happened to both of you? You are a mere speck of dirt in the eyes of the morcoug. Your sword could never reach its throat. I can't believe you endangered yourself and Cylena in this manner."

Taylith, who had left, returned, carrying the team on his dragon body. They slid down his neck, his leg, until they stood on the ground.

Icaras ran to Cylena and pulled her into a hug, then stepped back and shook his head. Biryn felt himself shriveling under his anger. "What were you thinking?"

Brenn stalked up to Biryn. "You scared us witless with your disappearance act. Thank the gods for Rania. She warned Ciara what you and Cylena are up to."

"You realize you were being a knucklehead pulling such a stunt?" Erica put in her bit.

Laro stood beside Erica and shook his head. "What did you just call the king?"

Erica grinned sheepishly. "I'll explain later."

"That is enough admonishment for now. Biryn realizes he put the fear of the gods in us. Now, how about you tell us about your vision, Cylena?" Ciara sat on a mossy patch and motioned the others to do the same.

CHAPTER TEN

After Cylena had told them of her vision, they ate, drank some of their water, and talked.

"I don't get it. So now Cewrick is suddenly a good guy?" Erica uttered.

Ciara nodded. "Remember what Zohmes did to your crewmember, John. It appears he did the same to Cewrick for many centuries. Zohmes wants control of Ierilia. He wants the throne. After we defeated Cewrick and he was banished to Garissa Island, his memories returned because Zohmes had left the host. He knew then that Zohmes had inhabited his body and caused him to do everything he did. Zohmes and Odoxon managed to free him because they thought Cewrick would be an ally to them and using their combined magick, they would be stronger than ever. They did not realize that Cewrick was back to the man he once was."

"So why did Zohmes not possess Cewrick again?" Brenn wondered.

"Because that would bind Zohmes. When he possesses another body, it binds much of his own powers. Each time he chooses a host, when he wants to cause havoc, like the hurricane, he has to leave that host for a brief period. That is why Erica's John appeared normal at times."

Astiana brushed her hair out of her face. "These are my thoughts. When Zohmes possessed Cewrick, magick users had practically destroyed each other in their quest for more power. After enslaving the jewel dragons, Zohmes possessed two very powerful sorcerers. He owned the body of Cewrick and the soul of King Brokig. This allowed him to merge their collective powers. There was no one left free that had the strength to defeat him, and there was no reason to leave his host... Until we defeated Cewrick."

Laro cleared his throat. "Mm, so now we are all here. We go and rescue the evil sorcerer?"

Ivran chuckled. "I cannot imagine my life without some crazy quest to fulfill. What a dull existence I led prior to joining the team and your troops, Biryn."

Aldis jumped up. "I can agree with that. It is time to move on. Is everyone ready?"

Biryn held his hand out to Cylena. "Love, as you can see, the team is here to help us."

She lowered her eyes and stared at the ground. "If they had not arrived, we would be dead by now. I should have listened to you and allowed you to contact them. I should have told Icaras."

"Yes, you should have. We can thank the goddess Rania for her intervention." He helped her with her backpack and taking her hand, pulled her along to follow the others.

"I am right behind you," Icaras growled.

"Icaras, I didn't think you would understand, and for that I am sorry," Cylena said over her shoulder.

"On the ship, I saw Cewrick, just as you did. I was given the same vision but chose to ignore it. After everything he did, what I had to live through because of him, killing our mother, attempting to kill you when you were born, I find it hard to believe that it was Zohmes controlling him. But I would have helped you, Cylena. No matter how I feel about him. You only had to ask."

"Enough," Biryn ordered. "Let us continue with the mission. The sooner we infiltrate the castle and rescue your father, the better. I have no wish to tarry near Odoxon's realm."

They climbed up the steep slope, encountering no more predators. Birds flew, small animals darted, but their path seemed clear. No brush or overgrowth of foliage hindered their progress. Suddenly, a bird scurried from a tree above them.

"Oh, look at that pretty bird." Cylena pointed at it.

"That is an aiah bird. They are very rare," Brenn pointed out.

The bird fluttered above them. White feathers covered its tiny body. A ring of shimmering mauve encircled its neck. The same mauve colored the center of its wings and long, lacy tail, blending to silver at the tips of the feathers. Its song surrounded them suddenly, notes so sweet, it would have melted ice.

Biryn sighed in pleasure when Cylena suddenly began to sing along softly. The magick of her voice had kept him anchored to the realm of the living while he was ill. Her melodious song softly filled the air, the purity of her voice calming them. It was as if she were in tune with the bird. The bird swooped down, pecked at her hair, then flew back up and disappeared.

"That was mesmerizing," Erica commented.

"Our mother had the same beautiful voice." Icaras' voice cracked.

Biryn knew what it was like to lose his parents, but the pain for Icaras had to be excruciating. Cewrick had tormented Icaras from the time he was born—his treatment at the sorcerer's hands had been abominable. First killing the people closest to Icaras, then cursing him into a worm and exiling him to the bowels of the planet for centuries. Thankfully, Rania had rescued Cylena, and she had been raised with people that cherished her.

They continued through the darkened forest along the path to the castle. The dense foliage above them blocked the light of the late evening suns. Fatigue slowed everyone down. The previous night's events had taken a toll on them. Biryn could feel his steps slowing as he forced himself to continue up the steep, rocky slope.

He gripped Cylena's arm and steadied her as she stumbled beside him. "You look as if you are asleep on your feet, little songbird." He shouted to the team. "We need to make camp. We could all use some rest."

Cylena's mouth twisted into a wry smile. "I should have listened to you, but I am so worried for my father. I can't leave him to be tortured by Zohmes and Odoxon."

"Now he knows what it feels like," Icaras growled.

"There is an outcropping of rocks up ahead. We'll stop there and use it for shelter," Aldis called out.

Biryn helped Cylena take off her backpack after they reached the rocks. He thanked the gods they at least had it to shelter beneath. There were large boulders on either side, affording them protection from possible predators. In their haste to leave, he hadn't thought about packing essentials other than the small amount of food and water he had grabbed before taking off in the flyer. He didn't even have a blanket for Cylena to sleep upon. He was angry at himself for coming so unprepared, but how else would they have left the palace quietly? He could not have gone to the kitchens. But forgetting their bedrolls was inexcusable. Although that would really have made the guards sound the alarm. Since the assassination attempts, his guards followed him everywhere if the team was not present.

Icaras threw two bedrolls to Biryn. "Brenn packed supplies for the both of you. He knew you couldn't have had time to prepare properly before you left so stealthily."

"Thank you, Icaras." He laid out the bedrolls and gestured for Cylena to sit down on one, then handed her some of the food and water he had packed. "Eat and rest, my love. I need to speak with the team. I will be back soon."

Cylena took a drink from the waterskin. "Thank you, Biryn."

Biryn joined the others at the fire Ivran had started and sat down by Astiana. He contemplated his group of friends a moment before speaking. He knew they had a right to be angry with him. They had risked their lives many times over to keep him safe and protect the crown. "I am sorry I didn't tell you what we were planning, but I couldn't let Cylena leave on her own. She is convinced of Cewrick's innocence, and oddly, I am beginning to believe that what she has said is true. It makes a lot more sense that Zohmes was the mastermind behind Cewrick's actions."

"I recall him shouting for Zohmes when we defeated him. Maybe that wasn't a cry for the bastard's help, but rather a cry of frustration as his memories returned and realization of everything he'd done began to sink in." Brenn took a bite of his bread.

"I agree, Brenn." Astiana patted Biryn's arm. "And I think all of us have made foolish decisions when it comes to the people we love."

Aldis pushed a chunk of meat onto a stick and held it over the fire. "Now that we are all involved in this reckless scheme, we need to come up with a plan. Scaling the mountain is the safest bet to get us to the castle unseen, but we do not have the proper equipment to climb safely."

"Ciara and I can fly everyone to the summit, but we will need to do it after nightfall. Rania told Ciara that Zohmes had released his favorite pets, the urcals, along with Cewrick. They guard Odoxon's castle," Taylith informed them.

"We need to rest for a short while. I did get some sleep before the summons to the palace, so I will stand guard and will wake you when it is time." Brenn sat on the ground near the entrance of the rock outcrop.

Biryn hastened to Cylena with a chunk of roasted meat for her. He found her curled up in the bedroll, fast asleep. He smiled. She looked so innocent and vulnerable as she lay there, her hair spread around her like a cloak. Undoing the strings of his bedroll, he placed it beside her and lay close to his sweet love, but he could not find sleep immediately.

Biryn suddenly felt his body change. He reached for Cylena, but she was not there. Nothingness. An empty void. Cylena! No sound came from his lips. He tried to jump up, but his body felt weighed down by lead. He looked at his surroundings. Darkness. A musty smell drifted to his nostrils. Slowly, his eyes became accustomed to the dark interior. Where am I? What happened? Where are the others? He was inside a dank, dark cave. Slimy mucous dripped from the walls. Strange creatures scurried along the dirt floor. Creaking. He looked toward the sound and saw a barred gate slowly open. Two hooded figures entered and walked toward the far wall. One of them carried a torch.

The torch lit up the figure of a naked man chained to the wall, his body covered by cuts, welts, and bruises. His face bloodied. A soft moan escaped from swollen lips. As one of the robed figures held up the torch, the other one produced a squirming fuplor. The lizard-like creature attached itself to the victim's chest and began to eat away at his skin and flesh. The man screamed, the sound piercing Biryn's heart. The man's eyes rolled back into his head, showing only the whites. Biryn realized he was witnessing Zohmes and Odoxon torturing Cewrick.

A woman appeared. Cylena? How? Had she gone on to the castle without him? Had Zohmes abducted her? She looked lovely, dressed in a white gown. One of them, he could not tell if it was Zohmes or Odoxon, threw the torch to the ground. He grabbed Cylena and ripped the fuplor off the man's chest, then placed it on Cylena's face. She fell to the floor, writhing. Her hands tore at the creature. After she'd ripped it off, half her face was missing.

"Nooooo! Get away from her!" Biryn, his stomach sickened, yelled and attempted to stand to get to her, but his shackles prevented him.

"Biryn, wake up. Biryn…"

He opened his eyes to see Cylena bending over him. Her face was intact. Sitting upright, he pulled her into his arms. "You are all right."

"Yes, of course I am. You had a bad dream." Her hand on his forehead soothed his shattered nerves.

Astiana approached them. "Biryn, you had a vision?"

"Yes. I was in a dungeon with Cewrick. We need to hurry. The torture they are inflicting upon him is terrible. They are using fuplors."

Brenn had joined them. "Fuplors? They are deadly. Tell us about your vision, Biryn, but come sit by the fire."

Biryn noticed everyone was awake and they seemed ready to move on but were having a quick snack and a drink. He stood, took Cylena's hand, and headed for the fire.

While they had some bread, cheese, and water, Biryn told them of his vision. "It was sheer horror. Cylena was not exaggerating when she told us of the torture inflicted upon the man. If we do not hurry, he will surely die."

Ciara shook her head. "No. They do not want him gone. They will keep him barely alive until he tells them what they want to know, or until he agrees to partner with them."

"If all of you have finished eating, let us pack up and get ready to leave," Brenn ordered and began to throw dirt on the fire to extinguish it.

"There is a clearing just behind the trees. We will need to go there to call out our dragons." Ciara motioned Taylith to follow her and disappeared into the darkness of the forest.

CHAPTER ELEVEN

The two dragons landed close to the forest line, far enough away from the massive wall surrounding the castle to keep from being sighted. One by one the team slid to the ground. Ciara and Taylith called out their humans and quickly joined the group. Hiding among the trees and brush of the forest line, they scrutinized the wall and the solid iron gates. Urcals perched atop the wall, many of them, like battlements along the top of a castle wall. Two grotesque guards stood before the weathered gate, holding colossal spiked clubs and maces. Biryn had never seen such ugly men—if one could even call them that. They did not look human. Their heads kind of resembled that of an urcal, with sharp, curving beaks and glowing red eyes, yet they had the semblance of a human body, had arms and legs. Ierilian men were normally tall. The Yeavoth people were giants, but these creatures would dwarf even them.

"It is impossible to approach the gates without the guards or the urcals seeing us," Biryn commented.

"We will take care of them. Wait here," Ciara and Taylith said in unison and swiftly shifted back to their dragons.

Awed, as always, by their beauty, visible even in the

darkness of the night, Biryn watched as they zoomed into the sky. Their scales shimmered in the moonlight, Ciara's a beautiful mauve hue, while Taylith's were the blue of an azure ocean.

The urcals never had the time to react and retaliate as the two dragons swooped in with the speed of lightning, fire issuing from their mouths. Flying around the castle, they obliterated each and every one of the huge birds. Then they took care of the two giants guarding the gate.

"Zohmes and Odoxon will surely know now that we are here," Astiana mumbled.

"Not necessarily. Those monsters hardly had time to sound the alarm. Taylith's and Ciara's attack on them may have seemed long to us, but they annihilated them all in just minutes. Look, they have landed near the gates and are waiting for us." Brenn motioned them forward.

"We need the four swords to open the gates," Astiana told them.

Biryn, Erica, and Brenn drew their swords and joined Taylith. Each placed their sword's blade against the doors, all four points touching each other. Biryn felt the power of his sword, the magick flowing from it into his body. The swords sparked, then hummed softly as if sawing through the thick iron. With a loud click, the doors opened enough for them to pass through.

"Eyes front, back, and sides," Aldis hissed. "There will be guards everywhere."

Biryn had expected a flurry of activity within the walls. It was probably as Astiana had said. Zohmes and Odoxon did not think the fortress could be accessed, that it was impenetrable, and without any warning sounded, they were hopefully asleep. But they still had to deal with the guards in the courtyard, the ones guarding the castle doors, and within the castle itself. It was not going to be easy. Taylith and Ciara could not call out their dragons here. The alarm would surely go off immediately.

The courtyard was deserted except for two guards at the castle's doors. They looked different from the two outside the wall. They were shorter and had green reptilian heads. They stood on two feet and had arms and legs, but their hands were more like claws and green, like their heads. They wore some kind of bronze armor, and each held a tall spear.

Brenn and Aldis led the group, approaching stealthily along the wall of the castle. Biryn held Cylena's hand in a firm grip, his sword in his other hand, ready for anything that might attack. They stopped just below the side wall of the stone steps.

Icaras and Ciara held hands and commenced to chant. Biryn watched as the reptilian guards turned to stone. He shuddered. It reminded him of the stone statue curse Cewrick had bespelled Ierilia with. But had it been Cewrick?

"Be ready for anything behind those doors," Brenn warned as he started up the steps, followed by Aldis, Ivran, and Laro. At the top, Brenn carefully took the large iron ring in his hands and turned it. The door opened easily.

"That seems almost too simple," Erica muttered.

They all stood at the top of the steps now. Biryn touched one of the reptilian statues gingerly and quickly withdrew his hand. One by one they quietly stepped through the half-open door into the hall. The interior smelled musty, old, like decaying paper. He recalled a time, centuries ago, before holographs, tablets, and technology, how there were libraries with ancient books. He believed many of the books were still in existence in their museum of Ierilian history, preserved within oxygen-free glass containment.

"No one. It is as if the castle is devoid of life," Taylith

commented in a whisper while advancing into the hall.

"Biryn, concentrate. You, too, Cylena, Ciara, and Icaras. Link hands. Rania will show us the door to the dungeons," Astiana told them, her words barely audible.

The five joined hands and closed their eyes. After a few seconds, they separated. Biryn pointed to a door not far from the entrance. "That is the one." The others nodded.

The door opened to a spiral stone staircase. Sconces were lit along the stone walls, the torch flames throwing eerie shadows over the walls and steps and the cobwebs hanging from the ceiling. The steps were narrow, crumbling in places. Biryn steadied Cylena as she almost tripped when a step began to collapse beneath her feet.

The stairs seemed to go down a long way. Vermin scurried out of their path, and spiders crawled along the walls. When they finally got to the bottom, they faced a large area that had several barred cells. One lone guard sat sleeping at a rickety old table. He looked much like the reptile guards at the door to the castle. Ciara and Icaras finished him off fast.

Brenn took a torch out of a sconce and walked up to each of the cells. All were empty but the last one. Brenn held the torch up, and Biryn saw Cewrick hanging against the wall, his manacles and chains taut. He appeared to be unconscious. He looked just like the man in his vision, except worse. Blood slowly seeped from the wounds inflicted upon him. His face was hardly recognizable.

Ciara rushed to him, a vial of her tears in her hands. Cylena almost broke his fingers, she squeezed so hard, while they watched Ciara apply her magick.

Icaras, his face a mask of disbelief, stood back. Biryn knew that the young man was still unsure of the man who had caused him so much pain.

Cewrick moved, opened his eyes and gazed at them. "I am

dreaming? This is a hallucination?"

Ciara placed her hand on his brow. "No, Cewrick. We are here to rescue you. Are you able to stand now?"

He straightened his legs and stood. Ciara touched each of his manacles. They opened, freeing his wrists and ankles. Finally, she touched the iron band around his neck. It released, now dangling from the chain.

Holding the vial to his lips, Ciara said, "Drink this. It will heal you."

"My powers. They are gone. Zohmes and Odoxon—"

Biryn stepped forward. "Cewrick, we can talk later. Take this blanket to cover yourself."

He gratefully took the blanket from Biryn's hands. "I do not know what to say. How to thank you all."

"We need to leave here. Now! Zohmes and Odoxon are on their way to the dungeons," Astiana told them. "Link hands. The rest of you stand in our circle."

Ivran and Laro supported Cewrick. Just as they began to chant, torches illuminated the dungeon entry. They heard a loud shout. Biryn saw Odoxon throw off his hood and hold up a gnarled black staff to point it at them. Lightning issued from the black crystal skull at its tip, but his attempt to stop them came too late.

"Why are we at the Clyss?" Biryn asked in surprise as they stood on the soft, silvery sand beside the magick pool.

"Cewrick needs more healing than my tears can give him. Though the healing properties are powerful, there was too much harm inflicted upon him." Ciara held her hand out to Cewrick. After he took it, she removed the blanket and led him to the pool. "You must enter the basin."

Cewrick stopped in his tracks. "But the monster—"

"That monster was me. You bound my dragon to this

pool."

Cewrick's shoulders slumped, and a pained expression crossed his features. "It was not me. I am sorry for what was done to you. The pool is harmless?"

Ciara tugged his hand, urging him to enter the water. "The pool will heal you completely. Enter it."

Cewrick stepped into the water until his head disappeared under the surface completely. He was submerged much longer than Brenn and Ciara had been at their joining ceremony.

Biryn was concerned that Cewrick had been beneath the surface too long. They hadn't just rescued the man to have him die in the Clyss. "He has been under a long time! Are you sure he has not drowned?"

Ciara smiled. "No. All the gods and goddesses are communicating with him right now and restoring his health and his powers. He will be fine."

Relieved, Biryn turned to Cylena. Her hand grasped his so tightly he was sure she had cut the circulation off to his fingers. He wondered if his hand would be still usable after this mission. "Your father will be fine, my love." He tucked a lock of her hair behind her ear, then faced the others. "After he is healed, we will return to my palace. Brenn, contact Trevain to retrieve my flyer."

Cewrick finally emerged and walked out of the pool toward them. Ciara hurried to drape a blanket around him. Cylena let go of his hand and took a step toward her father. For moments he stood, looking at them all. Then slowly he slid to the ground.

CHAPTER TWELVE

Biryn gathered Cylena into his arms. "I know you are anxious to face your father, but the man is exhausted after his ordeal. We are all very tired. You will see him tomorrow."

She kissed him and snuggled close. "Have I thanked you yet?"

"Yes, many times. Enough. Go to sleep. That's an imperial order!" He grinned at her and doused the lights.

Her hand traveled from his chest to the back of his neck. She pulled him toward her and whispered against his lips, "If I am to be your queen, then you are not allowed to give me imperial orders."

Those sweet words. It was an assent he craved, had starved to hear to the very depths of his being. For a lifemate bond to ever be completed, she had to accept every aspect of who he was. Not just the man, but also their destiny. His hands trembling, he cupped the back of her head, capturing her lips with his, devouring her with his kiss.

Cylena met his ardor with a hunger as voracious as his own. Breaking their kiss, she climbed on top of him, straddling his hips, her long white nightgown riding up her legs and exposing the satiny skin of her thighs. His heart pounded hard against his ribs. His cock throbbed with the need to fulfill their joining. He grasped her hips, holding her still, keeping her from brushing against his aching erection.

She leaned down and placed one hand on each side of his head. Her gaze locked with his, her stormy eyes dark with passion. "I love you, Biryn. Yes... A thousand times, yes! Now that I know my blood is not tainted by evil, I will be your queen."

Gods, she was a test to his self-control. When had she become so bold? He closed his eyes and took a deep breath to calm the raging fire burning within him. A promise had been made, and he would be damned if he broke it. He shifted her to the mattress. Gathering her in his arms, he kissed her tenderly, holding his passion in check. "You have made me the happiest man alive. I love you, my little songbird."

"Biryn—"

He placed his finger across her luscious lips. "I gave you my word, Cylena, and by the gods, it is taking all my strength of will to restrain myself."

Her hand slid across his chest, down his abdomen. Her fingers brushed the hem of his nightshirt, slipping beneath the material to caress his heated skin.

"Then do not."

A groan escaped him. Stilling her hand, he studied her face. He would love to give in, to lose himself in her arms, her body. He kissed her cheek. "Cylena, my love. I made a promise to you. Please...don't make me break it. Our joining will be that much sweeter because of it."

Cylena gazed at him, hunger burning brightly in her eyes. "I have lived for centuries. I am not so innocent as to not know what goes on between a man and a woman, and I ache for you. Now, I cannot wait. Seven days, Biryn. We will have our ceremony in seven days." She smiled at him. *"That* is an imperial order."

Hours later, they sat around Biryn's dining table, enjoying breakfast. He noticed Icaras was very quiet. So was Cewrick. Casually, trying not to be obvious, he studied the man. Gone was the aggressive countenance he had always displayed. His face was kind, no longer twisted by hatred. He hardly resembled the terrifying sorcerer they had known for so long. There was a slight resemblance to his two children, mainly the eyes and their dark raven hair. Icaras and Cylena both had Hirsuta's facial features. The guilt he must be feeling, knowing every horrible deed he'd committed, had to be tormenting him. Sure, it had been Zohmes using his body, but the knowledge still had to be destroying his soul. *Knowing he had killed the mother of his children, the woman he loved?* Biryn squeezed Cylena's hand. The knowledge had to be unbearable.

"Cewrick, now that we are gathered here around my table, please know that I have come to regard all the ones present as my family. If you wish to talk, whatever you say will remain in this room and with us." Biryn looked directly into the man's stormy eyes—eyes that held so much anguish it was staggering.

Cewrick took a sip from his wine and set his glass on the table. He directed his words to Cylena first, his voice hoarse with emotion. "My daughter, I will begin with an apology to you. There is nothing I can say that could ever undo what I attempted after your birth. When I set eyes upon you in that ship, my heart almost stopped. For a moment I thought my Hirsuta stood before me." Cewrick's body trembled, tears spilling from his eyes. He reached up and wiped them away.

"I realized then you were the infant that I—or I should say

Zohmes, threw into the raging torrents of the river. I can't bear the thought of what would have happened to you if the goddess Rania had not saved you, and I am forever grateful for it. Believe me when I tell you this. When Hirsuta informed me that she was carrying not one but *two* babies, I was beside myself with joy."

Cylena grasped Cewrick's hand and squeezed. "I know it was not you, Father. Why would Zohmes do such a thing?"

Cewrick patted her hand and shifted in his chair to look at both Cylena and Biryn. "Hirsuta and I knew Cylena was Biryn's lifemate before she was born. It was decreed in the book of knowledge and shared with us by Rania. Zohmes thought to kill her while she was an infant, before she came into her powers, to ensure his great-grandson would never have an heir."

Gods, what a tangled web, but the emotion...the grief pouring from Cewrick could not be faked. Biryn knew the man was telling the truth. That Zohmes had possessed his soul, body, and mind for centuries.

Icaras sat beside his father, his jaw clenched, his back ramrod straight. "How do we know you are telling us the truth now?" He brushed his hand through his hair and gazed at Cylena, his eyes filled with turmoil. "I cannot reconcile this new Cewrick with the father who mistreated me during my youth, the father that cursed me and cast me out when I was just a child. You cannot be washed clean of all you have done."

Taylith cast Icaras a penetrating look and gestured to Cewrick. "This man is not the same being that bound my soul as an abomination for centuries, Icaras. If he were, I would have run him through with my sword the moment I set eyes upon him."

Cewrick looked at Icaras beseechingly. "My son, I had no

knowledge of what I did. My body was not my own, my mind controlled by Zohmes. It feels as if I have been in a deep sleep for centuries and then I woke up on Garissa Island and learned the truth of it all."

Biryn cleared his throat. "When did Zohmes possess you?"

Cewrick looked defeated. He turned his attention back to Biryn. "Not long before the birthing of the twins. I cannot give you an exact time. Gods, I was so happy, very much in love with my mate, with Hirsuta. We looked forward to raising our children together." He smiled wistfully. "The last thing I remember is lying beside her in our bed. I felt you both kick against my hand as I laid it on her belly. Her head rested on my shoulder, and we talked about the babies and were planning our future before we drifted off to sleep."

"Do you remember the date?" Cylena asked.

"Yes. It was the night of full moons, a week before the start of winter."

Biryn calculated on his datapad. "That would be the night before the twins were born."

"I recall Hirsuta complaining about an ache in her back." Cewrick rubbed the nape of his neck. "Everything Zohmes did in my name has been revealed to me, and it has shredded my soul and will haunt me for centuries and will follow me even into the realm of dreams. Zohmes coveted the throne, still covets it, and thought he could use me to destroy the crown. How can I ever forgive myself for what he did to Hirsuta? I was supposed to protect her…and my children."

"What *did* you do to our mother?" Icaras demanded.

"She stood before me, beseeching me to be kind, to stop tormenting my son. She begged me to forgo my evil magick. Of course, she was begging Zohmes, not me. He became very angry. He had found out about the powerful magick Icaras was blessed with by Rania and had no use for Hirsuta once the secret was out. Before my eyes, she disintegrated into a strange vortex of smoke and flames. She was gone. I can't erase the vision of it from my mind. I didn't know what was happening then. I couldn't stop him."

"That is what he did to me! It did not kill me. I found myself in Yanata, chained to a wall!" Cylena said excitedly. "My mother could still be alive!"

Shock crossed Cewrick's face. "Zohmes did that to you?"

"Yes. We will tell you everything later. Biryn and his team saved me."

Icaras almost threw his fork on his plate. "I remember when you told me that my mother was dead. You were so cruel. Your words cut me to the core. Claiming that she was an unnecessary obstacle in my life, that she had made me weak and I needed her no longer. How can you tell a child such things? And yet, I longed for your approval. And what did I get as reward?"

There was a chasm between Cewrick and Icaras that Biryn didn't think would ever be filled. Not that he blamed Icaras for his disbelief in Cewrick's innocence. Icaras had been cursed at fifteen and left to rot alone for centuries. All he had ever known as a father was Zohmes in Cewrick's body.

"Son, it was not me. What Zohmes did to you, how he used my body and our combined magick, is abominable. I can never repair the abhorrent evil he sowed. And now he has the help of Odoxon, and he still wants the throne. There is no stopping that revolting god, or Odoxon."

"But we must stop them both," Biryn responded. "What you told us about Hirsuta is more than interesting. Could she possibly be alive somewhere? Held by Zohmes?"

Astiana answered him. "We can talk to Rania. If it is written in the book of knowledge and Rania is allowed to tell us, we will know."

112

Cewrick slammed his fist on the table, startling them all. "The book of knowledge. You must rescue Niqine before Zohmes and Odoxon get to her."

"Yes, you told us in the ship. Niqine is safe. No one can enter the Tideless Abyss, except those allowed by the gods." Brenn wiped his mouth with a napkin.

"Now, before we discuss anything else, any future missions, there is something I would like to announce." Biryn clasped Cylena's hand in both of his. "Cylena and I are betrothed. She will be my queen. I would like the announcement to be broadcasted far and wide so that all of Ierilia hears this happy news."

"Oh, wow. A wedding coming up!" Erica lifted her glass. "A toast to the happy couple."

After they all took a sip of their wine, Biryn continued. "Our joining will be held a week hence in the Clyss. The celebration is to be held here, at the palace. All heads of the realms will be sent invitations. All people from Earth must attend. The invitations will be transmitted today, and preparations will begin."

"That is fast, Biryn, for such a huge event," Brenn warned.

"Yes. Cylena and I have decided we do not want to wait. She has led a lonely existence for centuries, and so have I. Besides, we are lifemates. There is no reason for us to delay." He grinned broadly and said, "And we need an heir to the throne as you have all mentioned several times."

Icaras seemed a bit disgruntled. "I am happy for you both, but my sister and I have spent very little time in each other's company since we found her. It is very fast, Biryn."

"Icaras, you are welcome to take up residence in the palace and spend time with Cylena while I attend to my kingly duties. I am sure Cewrick will want to return to his castle."

"Right. I had forgotten that now he is back and going

unpunished for his crimes, the castle is his."

"Icaras, stop," Cylena softly admonished.

"I understand your feelings, Icaras." Cewrick held out his hand to his son. "Please, I can never make up to you what you endured, but can we begin anew?"

Icaras ignored the hand and toyed with his food. "I will think about it."

"Dunmore, can you send out the invitations forthwith?" Biryn turned to his new aide.

"Yes, Sire. Immediately."

The conversation proceeded to the upcoming joining and celebration and took on a much happier note. Even Cewrick participated.

Cewrick held up his goblet. "Biryn, to see my daughter wed the king of Ierilia will light up some of the darkness and anguish now inhabiting my heart and soul. I am so grateful to see both my children alive and well. It is a salve on wounds that will fester and plague me for many years."

Erica held up her datapad. "Dunmore is fast. I am already receiving communications from my crew and the other people from Earth. They are excited. Cylena, one of the crew of the Initiation One, Olivia Porter, is a seamstress and designer. I remember some of the beautiful dresses she designed on Earth. She asks if she can have the honor of designing your gown and those of your bridesmaids as she's extremely grateful for the king's acceptance of her and the crew."

"Bridesmaids?" Cylena asked, frowning.

"Your attendants. If you plan to have any of course."

"I think so. I will need help to plan our joining. Ciara, Astiana, and Erica?" She looked questioningly at Biryn.

"Whoever you wish, my love. I am not sure about the seamstress from Earth. I do not wish to insult the palace seamstress. It is Cylena's decision. Brenn, Ivran, Laro, Aldis, Taylith, and Icaras, you will stand by me. That means you are short three attendants, Cylena."

"Oh. How about your doctor, Catrice? She saved your life. And Laura? Oh, and Kira? Yes, I have decided. Erica, please summon Olivia Porter to the palace? The palace seamstress can assist her as it is a big task to sew that many dresses in seven days."

CHAPTER THIRTEEN

Biryn paced back and forth in his rooms. He had not been with Cylena that night, and he would not see her now until he arrived at the Clyss. The week had been crazy. The whole palace had become a madhouse after the announcement of the betrothal. He was sure all the royal staff members had lost their minds. "How long before we depart for the Clyss, Dunmore?"

"Not long now, Sire. Your attendants are all waiting for you."

Biryn was nervous. His heart pounded, blood raced, and he couldn't stop the pacing. Thankfully, the week had passed quietly. What if Zohmes had something planned to upset the celebrations of that day? He recalled what had happened the night of Laro and Erica's joining. He prayed silently and begged the gods and goddesses to watch over them, to allow the ceremony and celebration to go uninterrupted. "Let us go to the other room and join the team."

Dunmore opened the door for him. Though his heart was torn at what had happened to Raollin, he was very happy with his new aide. At least Dunmore did not fuss over him the way Raollin had always done, but he had been so much more than an aide. Raollin was his friend, and he would be greatly missed. Dunmore was efficient, courteous, always ready to assist. He also had double duty as his personal guard and piloting his flyer.

"There he is!" Brenn shouted and held up his goblet. "Are you ready for this day, Biryn?"

"I am. More than you realize. My only fear is that Zohmes and Odoxon will interfere."

"We have all prayed to the gods and goddesses that this event will have no intrusions," Taylith assured him.

"You all look very grand," Biryn complimented his team. He perused them. At Cylena's insistence, Olivia had designed his own finery. But he had insisted the men dress in their formal blue uniforms, so he'd had the palace seamstress make uniforms for Taylith and Icaras. At least that way the woman hadn't felt completely left out. Cylena had also insisted he not wear a uniform.

"As do you, Biryn. The Earth seamstress did very well in her design of your joining ensemble." Aldis pointed at the mirror. "The colors match our uniforms very well."

He stood before the tall mirror and gazed at his reflection. The color of his tunic was an exact match to the blue of the uniforms. Delicate gold embroidery from the neck to mid-chest and across the shoulders. A gold-pleated sash held the tunic around his waist. At the wrists and the bottom, the same delicate embroidery finished the tunic off. The seamstress had placed the royal emblem, a crown held by two dragons, just over his hip. His pants were black, as were his above-the-knee boots. A blue velvet cloak lined with gold silk and edged with gold filigree draped from his shoulders. How Olivia had managed to design and get all the clothing ready in time was a mystery to him. Maybe she had worked together with the palace seamstress? She had to have had help. All that fine embroidery. There was no way one person could have readied all of it in time.

"Sire, your crown." Dunmore held the crown above Biryn's head.

"Thank you. Brenn, do you have Cylena's crown?"

"Yes. I do. It is time to go. You do not want to be late for this."

Clyss Valley was filled to the brim with guests. The Earth crew alone numbered many, plus all the rulers of the various realms, along with family and friends. He had never seen so many people gathered there. They all stood and clapped as he walked toward the pool and took his position. His six attendants stood beside him.

Biryn's heart thumped when the flyer carrying Cylena and her entourage landed.

She walked toward him, Cewrick on one arm and Rimog, her adoptive father, on the other. A soft murmur sounded from the guests as they saw the sorcerer. He did not care. Right now, his focus was on Cylena, her beauty so great on this day, he almost forgot to breathe.

Her white dress was otherworldly, a gown such as Ierilia had never seen. The bodice accentuated her figure, her small waist. The sleeves to the elbow had lace cascading to the wrists. The full skirt was made of gossamer-fine material with small blue flowers and lacy greenery embroidered all over. An overskirt adorned by a lacy ruffle draped from just under the bodice. It elongated into such a long train that three of her attendants walked on each side, carrying it. Its edges were also embroidered with the same blue flowers and green leaves. A gossamer-thin blue cloak draped from her shoulders. Some of her hair had been braided into a coronet, the remainder hanging free in loose waves. Her eyes sparkled as she approached him, her cheeks flushed. He barely noticed the attendants except that their dresses were also elaborate and the same shade as the blue flowers on her dress.

"My king, please accept my daughter's hand." Cewrick's voice was hoarse with emotion as he took Cylena's hand and placed it on Biryn's.

He felt her hand tremble, looked down at her moist eyes, her lips forming a sweet smile. "I accept your daughter's hand, Cewrick of Sucronia."

Cewrick and Rimog stepped back to join the guests of honor.

White clouds appeared above the Clyss. A swarm of white, snowy birds flew over the guests, their song echoing through the valley. Sparkling particles rained down upon the couple. A man slowly descended from the clouds. The guests gasped. It was Izarus. His snow-white hair hung to his waist. Dressed in gold-and-white robes that fluttered around him as if there were a breeze, he looked very regal as he stood close to Biryn and Cylena. Rania, Asphine, and Astiana stood beside him, and a row of gods and goddesses on either side to witness this special event. His dragon-topped staff was gold. When he spoke, his deep voice boomed.

"I am Izarus. Ruler of all gods and goddesses. I have come here on this joyous day to personally unite this couple. Ierilia has not seen a royal joining in many centuries. This ceremony is a very special occasion where Biryn, ruler of all Ierilia, and Cylena, daughter of Cewrick of Sucronia and adoptive daughter of Rimog and Jaleah, will bind their lives together. Biryn and Cylena, please join hands and stand before me."

Biryn felt shaky as he took Cylena's hands in his. The appearance of Izarus was a complete surprise. He had expected Rania to perform the ceremony. Even more of a surprise were the gods and goddesses all attending.

"Biryn, do you take this woman as your mate? Will you

honor her and protect her always? Do you pledge before me, the gods and goddesses, and these witnesses that you will be her defender with all that you are?"

Biryn nodded. "I always will."

"Cylena, do you take this man as your mate? Do you pledge before me, the gods and goddesses, and these witnesses to honor Biryn? That you shall be his one true and lasting counselor and solace? Do you forsake all for him?"

"I will."

Brenn stepped forward and wound a red cord around their wrists, followed by Aldis, who bound their wrists with an ivory cord. Ciara stepped up to wind a gold cord around their wrists, followed by Astiana with a blue cord.

Izarus nodded to someone behind him. Rania approached them to tie the four cords together.

"These knots are tied so that your souls are now forever bound. Woven into these cords are the blessings of all the gods and goddesses that are witness to this great event. May your spoken vows never grow bitter in your mouths. Now place your hands on my staff."

With the cords still binding their wrists, Cylena and Biryn placed their hands on the golden rod. It began to glow, illuminating them in a soft light, and the dragon on top shone fiercely, surrounding the couple in a bright red glow.

"What has been joined together by me, Izarus, may never be undone by man. Before I proclaim you joined, you must kiss thrice while holding my staff."

Biryn bent and placed a gentle kiss on Cylena's waiting lips. Then two more. The soft tendrils of magick pulsed along his arm, up his shoulder, and burst through his body. Cylena's essence filled him, her soul entwining with his.

"By my power and the blessing of all gods and goddesses, I now proclaim you joined. May you lead a rich and fruitful life."

The cords disappeared from their wrists. The clouds dissipated, and the sky was again an azure blue. Izarus was gone, as were the gods and goddesses. Biryn heaved a sigh of relief as he pulled Cylena into his arms. "Now to crown you," he murmured against her lips.

Tears flowed freely down her cheeks now. "I feel so overwhelmed."

"I know, songbird. The crowning is the last part. It will not take long."

He held her at arm's length and nodded to Brenn. He approached them, holding a velvet cushion. Atop it rested a beautiful gold crown that was studded with blue and white jewels. Beside it, the royal scepter. Biryn took the crown off its soft bed, then stood before his mate.

"Cylena, will you accept this crown and be my queen?"

"Yes." Her answer was barely audible.

"I place this crown upon your head and pronounce you queen of Ierilia." After carefully placing the crown on her head, he took the scepter and touched it to both her shoulders, then her forehead.

"My queen," he murmured and kneeled before her, taking her hand in his. He tenderly kissed each of her fingers, then rose still holding her hand. He turned them to face the guests that filled the Clyss Valley. "I now introduce Cylena, queen of Ierilia."

A cry rose from the crowd, filling the valley with its joyous notes. "Blessings to the queen! Blessings to the queen! Blessings to the queen!"

CHAPTER FOURTEEN

Holding her in the shelter of his arms, Biryn waited until all the guests had left. When he had arrived, Biryn had not even noticed there was not a flyer or hovercraft parked in the Clyss. Now he realized, of course there could not have been. Not with that many guests. They had all been flown to the Clyss, and the crafts had departed and waited beyond the summit of the mountain.

"Everyone but you and I and our attendants has gone, my love. Now we go to the palace to celebrate."

"Biryn, Olivia designed and made such wonderful dresses for me and my attendants, but how can I enjoy myself in this gown?"

Erica laughed. "I'm with you on that one. I think we need to keep them on for a little while, though. Maybe just for the official dinner."

Biryn could finally admire the attendant's dresses. Though not as elaborate as Cylena's, they, too, were otherworldly. The material was the same color blue as the flowers on Cylena's gown and robe, and they were embroidered with tiny white flowers. The ladies all had a coronet of white flowers on their hair, and all looked lovely, but none could surpass the beauty of his queen. "There is my flyer. Shall we leave for the palace?"

Deep down, all he wanted was to whisk her off to his quarters and take her to his bed. He had to be patient. This promised to be a long evening. He did not look forward to the various speeches by all the rulers of the realms. But from what he had researched of past royal joinings, it was tradition, so they would have to sit through it all.

"Do I have to wear the crown all evening?" Cylena asked him softly at the dinner table.

"Only until after the dinner, love. Then we can go and change into comfortable clothing and enjoy the evening."

The dining hall now adjoined the ballroom and the throne room to accommodate the many tables for the guests. A sea of flowers decorated the whole castle, wafting their intoxicating scent throughout.

Biryn shifted in his seat. The speeches bored him to tears, though he knew they were all meant well. Just about all the rulers of the realms had to have their little say. It seemed endless. He was sure Cylena felt the same as he did, though she did not voice her feelings. She was very poised and royal in her mannerisms as if she were born a royal princess and had lived among royalty all her life.

All his subjects were ecstatic to see him with a queen. The gifts from all the rulers of his realms overflowed the tables in his throne room. Of course they had to acknowledge each gift and thank the gift giver. The best gift of all was that Zohmes and Odoxon had not disturbed their happy occasion. He silently thanked the gods and goddesses for that.

"What are we going to do with all those things, Biryn?" Cylena whispered near his ear.

He grinned and whispered back, "The treasury is already overfull. We will store them for now and later give most of them away to people that will make use of them. Like the people from Earth that have nothing, and Brenn's people. Everything they had was burned to the ground."

He was glad when the dinner finally came to an end. The staff began to clear the tables and take them away to empty the ballroom to get it ready for dancing. The guests stood around waiting while enjoying their wine. The orchestra had installed themselves on the stage and began playing their music. It didn't take long for them to clear the floor and guests began to dance. "We can go and get changed now," he told Cylena.

"I have my clothes ready. Olivia designed and made more than one gown for me," she told him.

He held his arm out for her. "Then allow me to escort you to your chambers to get comfortable, my love."

"This will be the last time I dress in the queen's chambers. From this night forth, I will be sharing your bedroom." She smiled up at him.

After they had changed, Biryn knocked on her door. She opened it and shyly walked toward him. She looked exquisite in a gown made of white silk. The form-fitting bodice had an intricate pattern of flowers and vines embroidered in gold thread. The skirt flared out at her hips and was just long enough for her gold sandals to peek through when she walked. A gold sash circled her hips, matching the gossamer veils at her shoulders. The necklace he had given her encircled her neck. Gods, he couldn't wait for this celebration to end. "Once again, you look beautiful beyond words. You were born to be a queen," he softly said while offering his arm.

They entered the ballroom to a round of cheers, the orchestra quickly changing their tune to the haunting melody of a traditional Ierilian joining song. He led her to the dance floor, pulled her close, and guided her. "You are the most beautiful woman I have ever seen, little songbird."

Cylena rested her head against his shoulder. "You make me feel treasured and beautiful, Biryn."

Biryn twirled her around the room, relishing the feel of her in his arms. He gazed at the people enjoying the celebration as they danced around the room. His team never strayed far from them, all of them strategically placed to protect them if Zohmes should initiate an attack. And yet they all seemed relaxed, enjoying the celebration. He couldn't help but grin when young Tomas pulled Erica to the dance floor. Not too far from them, Catrice danced with Mark.

Biryn noticed Erica pull away from Tomas and grab Catrice by the arm. A small commotion happened nearby, the dancers parting and crowding around a man who suddenly disappeared from his sight. Biryn's gaze followed Erica as she made her way between the spectators to a woman lying prone on the floor, the man kneeling beside her.

"Please, give us some space?" he heard Erica urge the people.

Biryn guided Cylena to the scene. "Is she okay? Erica, is this woman one of your crewmembers?"

"Yes. It is Julia, Laura's sister." Erica motioned to the man. "Samuel is from the Initiation Two." She turned to Samuel. "Can you tell us what happed?"

Samuel shook his head, a worried expression in his eyes. "I don't know. One minute we were dancing and the next she just fainted. I barely managed to catch her as she fell to the floor."

Erica patted Samuel's arm. "It's all right, Samuel. We will take care of her. You go ahead and enjoy the rest of the celebration."

"Julia, oh my God!" Laura rushed up beside them and

dropped to the floor by her sister, shaking her. "Julia, please, honey. Wake up. You don't think she was drugged, do you?"

Taylith stood behind Laura and gently squeezed her shoulder. "No, I don't think she has been drugged, at least not with bindweed."

Julia opened her eyes. She gazed at Laura, her face pale, a fine sheen of perspiration covering her upper lip. Her voice was weak as she spoke. "Laura?"

"We need to take her to my examination room." Catrice helped Julia sit up and quickly took her pulse. "Laura, sweetheart, let me take care of your sister. She will be fine."

Before Biryn could say a word, Taylith and Laro stepped in and carefully lifted Julia from the floor, supporting her between them. He quickly scanned the room. The rest of his team were calming the guests that had witnessed Julia fainting. It had been strained enough at the ceremony and during dinner with Cewrick present, though many of his subjects had relaxed and were enjoying themselves after the initial shock of seeing him. Biryn had come to terms with this new Cewrick. If he were still the evil man he once was when he was possessed by Zohmes, the gods and goddesses would never have allowed him into the Clyss and restored his powers.

Cylena squeezed his hand, startling him out of his thoughts. "I hope she will be okay."

"The doctor will take care of her. Maybe she consumed too much chairi wine. We will soon know."

Catrice led them to the examining room and small infirmary specially set up for her use in the palace. Taylith and Laro helped Julia sit on the examination table Catrice had pointed out, then stepped out of the room to join the rest of them in the waiting area.

A few moments later, Jason entered the infirmary along

with Ciara and Brenn. Jason knocked on the door of the examination room, entering when Catrice opened the door.

"Astiana and Icaras are acting as hosts in your stead. We do not believe this incident has anything to do with Zohmes." Ciara smiled at them. "Do not worry. The guests believe you have left the celebration for the evening, as is customary for a newly joined couple."

"Many of the guests are still present and enjoying the celebration, so Aldis, Ivran, and Mark have remained in the ballroom to provide extra security." Brenn turned to Cylena. "Your parents send their good wishes. Dunmore is returning them to Cewrick's castle."

Biryn glanced toward the examining room door as Jason stepped out, a vial of blood in his hand.

Laura jumped from her seat and rushed to Jason. "Is Julia okay? Does Catrice know what is wrong with her?"

Jason squeezed her shoulder. "Julia is going to be fine. Let me run the blood tests Catrice requested. She will be able to tell you what is wrong with your sister after we have the results."

"Thank you, Jason." Laura returned to sit beside Taylith.

Biryn didn't miss the dragon sliding his arm around the young woman when she leaned her head against his shoulder. Erica sat on the other side of Laura, holding her hand. He could feel the tension in the room as they impatiently waited for Jason to run the blood tests.

What seemed like an hour was only a few minutes. Jason returned from the lab, holding what Biryn knew was a bag of IV fluids in his hand. He cast them a bemused expression, then walked into the examination room. Several minutes passed before Catrice stepped out of the room, leaving the door open. Biryn could see Julia lying on the table. Jason was beside her, inserting the IV catheter into her vein, then

127

attaching the catheter to the tubing of the bag of fluids.

Catrice grinned at Laura. "Come on in, Laura, you can see your sister now."

Laura joined Catrice and entered the examination room, approaching the table.

Biryn heard the murmur of their voices as they spoke, then an excited squeal.

"Are you sure? But how? When? I can't believe you are pregnant, Julia!" Laura exclaimed excitedly, her voice carrying to the waiting area.

Biryn had no idea why Laura could possibly be excited about her sister's illness. *Pregnant? What kind of illness is that?* He didn't have to wonder long.

Erica blurted out the answer. "Oh my God! Julia is with child!"

Biryn cast a surprised glance around the room. Erica had a shocked expression on her face. But all Biryn felt was relief. There was no possible way Zohmes could be involved in this. Children were a gift from the gods. He hoped the gods would bless him and Cylena with many.

Catrice left the examination room and joined them in the waiting area. "I guess you have all heard the news?" She turned to Biryn. "If it is okay with you, I'd like to keep Julia overnight in the infirmary as a precaution. She thought she merely had an upset stomach, hasn't been able to keep anything down and is dehydrated. I'd like to monitor her overnight."

"Anything you need is at your disposal. We will leave it in your capable hands, Catrice." He looked at the others, still wondering about Erica's shocked expression, and now Ciara seemed troubled, too. He would find out tomorrow. Right now, all he wanted was to be alone with his queen.

"Cylena and I wish to retire for the night, but before we do,

I need to do one more thing. Erica, Laura, Catrice, Jason, please come to the ballroom? I need you to be present for this."

Laura frowned. "Is it important? I'd like to stay with my sister."

"I will stay with her, Laura," Taylith offered.

"She needs to rest for now. You can sit with her later, Laura." Catrice began to follow Biryn and Cylena.

"Do you know what this is about?" Erica whispered close to Ciara.

"I have no idea. We will soon find out."

They entered the ballroom, the dancers immediately clearing a path for the king and queen. Biryn steered Cylena to the raised platform and held up his hand to silence the band. A murmur sounded from the guests, all wondering why the music had stopped suddenly.

Biryn held up his free hand, his other squeezing Cylena's. A hush fell over the crowd. "Honored guests, staff, and people from Earth. The queen and I thank you from the depth of our hearts for helping to make this the most wonderful day of our lives. Thank you all so much for the bountiful gifts you have brought us. And thank you all for traveling from all corners of Ierilia to grace us with your presence.

"I especially wish to thank Olivia Porter and her assistants for creating our wonderful clothing in a mere week. Thank you for working night and day to help make my mate look the beautiful queen she was meant to be.

"I have not had the opportunity to welcome or meet many of our new people from the planet Earth. Welcome to Ierilia. The queen and I would like to grant you your own realm. When you have all learned the language and customs, you can begin, with our assistance, building your own city. What you name the realm has to be approved by the court. It will not be too far from here. There is a vast uninhabited realm not far from Cront, just beyond the Vlenill Mountains. The valley on the other side of those mountains is very fertile, and the realm has easy access to Cront through the Vlenill Pass. We will supply you with all you need to build and to travel. Please know, the realm, though with its own ruler, will fall under Ierilian law. Papers will be drawn up in the next few days, and my scribe will be in contact with whomever you choose as your ruler.

"Laro and Ivran, you have become family. For outstanding bravery and loyalty, we would like to grant you your own estates. There are two vacant estates not far from Cront. The former owner of one has traveled to the realm of dreams, and the owner of the other estate has moved to another realm with his family. The queen and I have acquired both for you.

"Now, please continue the celebration while the queen and I retire for the evening." He motioned to the band, and it began to play again.

"Come, songbird. I think it is time we made our escape."

CHAPTER FIFTEEN

Snow began to fall, but it did not deter his subjects from celebrating. Fireworks lit up the sky, coloring the snowflakes into sparkling gems. Music drifted into his quarters. The night was alive with the sounds of many happy people shouting and dancing in the streets of Cront, regardless of the weather. Their joining had been broadcasted throughout the planet.

Biryn paced the room, listening to it all while impatiently waiting for his mate. He wore nothing but a pair of loose lounge pants, and even with the chill in the air from the snowfall, his skin was heated, his body burning with an insatiable need he could not quench. Seven days of blissful torture had tested the boundaries of his resolve.

Hundreds of big, tall candles lit the room. The bed had been decorated with garlands of flowers, and bouquets of fragrant blossoms stood on the night tables and throughout the room. A bottle of chairi wine, along with two goblets, waited on a table beside the bed. He smiled. The staff had put a lot of effort into making this night magical for them. There was even a platter of fruit, cheese, and bread.

He stopped for a moment at his bedside table. Reaching for

his communicator, he turned it off. Nothing was allowed to disturb this night. He recalled the night of Erica and Laro's joining, how he had banged on their door in the middle of the night. *Oh, gods, nothing like that must happen this night. Please.*

The door opened and Cylena entered. His breath caught in his throat. His feet refused to move. All he could do was drink in the beauty that stood before him. She wore nothing but a sheer gown. Against the light of the candles, her shapely body was clearly visible through the translucent fabric. Her long black hair hung loose and cascaded in soft waves over her shoulders down her back. He gazed at her small, firm breasts, her dark aureoles and nipples teasing him through the thin material. He craved to touch, to taste every inch of her soft ivory skin. And by the gods, he could feel her. The hunger...the craving—just as voracious as his own—pulsed through the bond between them and it was electrifying.

The soft echoes of the music drifting through the windows from the celebrations outside changed to a slow, melodious tune. He strode quickly to her, taking her in his arms. "Dance with me, my beautiful queen?"

She gazed up at him, passion blazing in her eyes. "I would love to dance." She wrapped her arms around his neck, her body pushing against his. Her hips swayed seductively from side to side, brushing against him.

He leaned down, capturing her lips. She opened for his teasing assault, matching his ardor with her own, her tongue entering his mouth, exploring. He grasped the material of her nightgown, lifting it. Cylena stepped back and raised her arms, allowing him to remove her gown. His cock throbbed, aching for her. He picked her up and carried her to the bed, laying her gently on the downy comforter.

He couldn't take his eyes off her. Her raven hair splayed out around her, a dark contrast to the ivory of her skin. Those stormy gray eyes of hers glowed with her inner power…and desire. She was more than a queen. She was a goddess. *My goddess.* She held her hand out to him, beckoning him to join her. Who was he to resist?

He lay down beside her, gathering her into his arms. "I love you so much, Cylena." His voice was hoarse with desire. His lips sought hers. A taste…a tease, before moving to her jaw, her neck, down her chest to the peak of her breast, taking her nipple in his mouth. His trembling hand explored her creamy skin, stroking the underside of her neglected breast till his fingers reached her nipple and gently pinched the taut little peak. Her back arched, and her hands grasped the back of his head, a moan escaping her sweet lips. Her fingers drifted down his neck and shoulders, to his back, then stopped at the waist of his pants. Her hand dipped beneath the material. He groaned. Gods, the woman was testing his restraint.

She protested when he stilled her hand. "Biryn, please…I ache to touch you, too."

He glanced up at her passion-filled face. "Patience, my little songbird. I don't want to hurt you, nor do I want this to end too quickly." He gave her a lopsided grin. "You can have your way with me later."

She moved his hand back to her breast and smiled at him. "Then, by all means, let us continue, my king."

Her boldness stoked the fire burning within him. He looked forward to being at the mercy of her touch. He returned his attention to her tantalizing breasts, caressing and kneading them till her body writhed. He captured her lips in an ardent kiss, one hand teasing her nipple, the other smoothing down her sleek stomach and hips, seeking the slick wetness at the apex of her thighs. Her hips bucked when his fingers grazed the nub of her clit. Breaking their kiss, his mouth traveled the same path as his hand. Her body trembling beneath him, he explored every inch of her creamy skin, her taut stomach, the flare of her hips. He took her clit into his mouth, sucking and taunting the little bundle of nerves until her gasps of pleasure reached his ears. His fingers slid across her velvety folds, finding her core. He gently pushed one finger into her wet opening, stopping when he felt the barrier that would cause her pain on their joining.

He hated the thought that their making love this first time would hurt her, but he would temper that pain. His finger retreated, then pushed back in. A second finger joined the first, then a third, stretching her tight entrance. Her hips thrust with the movement of his hand, her sweet nectar flowing down his hand. A cry of pleasure escaped her, and her muscles clamped around his fingers.

He eased his way up her body, positioning his aching cock at her entrance. His eyes locked with hers, his body trembling as he forced the ravenous need down. Oh so slowly, he guided his cock into her, stretching her further. Gods, the pressure, the way her muscles fit snuggly around him, he felt as though he would burst.

Her hands snaked around him, her fingers caressing his shoulders, his back, then grabbing his ass. Her hips arched against him. "Now, my king...please... I am ready."

With one swift movement, he broke through the barrier as her body thrashed in the throes of her release. He was seated to the hilt, the walls of her pussy clamping around him like a warrior's glove. He stilled his body, not daring to move, worried he may have hurt her. He groaned as she shifted her hips, her hands kneading his ass, urging him on. He retreated and advanced again and again, building a rhythm of pleasure. Her body writhed beneath his, his name whispered from her lips as he drove them both over the precipice into blessed release.

He shifted beside her, pulling her tenderly into his arms. Gods, he couldn't believe it, no interruptions, no emergencies. He kissed her hesitantly on the lips. "I didn't hurt you?"

She caressed his jaw, love shining in her eyes. "Gods, no, Biryn. Far from it. Only pressure, then absolute joy."

He sighed in relief, hugging her tightly, then kissed the tip of her nose. "Let me draw us a bath, my sweet songbird."

He left the bed and hurried to the bathroom, turning the water on, allowing his large tub to fill. Returning to his bed, he lifted Cylena in his arms, carried her to the bath, and placed her on her feet beside it. He settled himself in the warm water and reached his hand out to her. She stepped into the warm, perfumed water and seated herself in front of him. Her back rested against his chest. They washed, splashed and played, relishing each other's company, unhindered for once by Zohmes' quest for the throne. After the water began to cool, rather than add more hot water, they dried quickly and returned to the comfort of their bed.

Biryn poured two glasses of chairi wine. He handed one to Cylena. "A toast to my beautiful mate." They clinked glasses, then took a sip of the sweet wine. She handed her glass back to him, and he set them on the night table. She cuddled close to him. "Wait, I have something for you."

Smiling, he grabbed a package from the table. It was a gift for his love, delivered to the palace only hours before their joining ceremony.

He handed the small package to Cylena. "Open it, my little songbird."

She looked up at him in surprise. "A gift? You have given me so much already."

"Not as much as you have given me, my queen. Open it."

Cylena opened the package, pulling out the music box he had one of his craftsmen design for her. It was exquisite in detail. Gold filigree covered the ivory box, sparkling blue gems embedded in gold decorating the sides and lid. Her name was engraved on the top, a tiny gold crown emblazoned above it. She lifted the lid, their reflections peeking back from the mirror inside. A crystal likeness of an aiah bird popped up, its wings glittering in the soft light of the candles. It had a long, feathery tail, just like the bird they had seen when going to Odoxon's castle. The soft melody of the aiah bird surrounded them.

She gasped, her hand covering her mouth. "Biryn, it is so beautiful! It takes my breath away. I will treasure this all my life."

He took the music box from her and placed it back on the bedside table. "I love you, songbird."

She snuggled into his arms and rested her head against his chest. "And I love you, my handsome king."

CHAPTER SIXTEEN

The campfire crackled as Biryn roasted his fish over the flames. It was their last day away. The day after the joining and celebration, he had decided to take his queen on a tour of Ierilia for seven days and had introduced her to the wonderful sights of various realms. They had spent the last four days on the warmer side of the planet, at the Chircaul Coast, camping on a secluded, private beach. How surprising that the last seven days had been uneventful.

He'd asked Brenn and Laro and their mates to accompany them, especially since neither had been able to enjoy their time with their women after their respective joining. The two warriors also served as their guards. They had been good about keeping their distance, giving them plenty of time alone. It had been a long time since he had visited the Chircaul Coast. He had explored every inch of the sandy beach as a child, but Cylena had never traveled farther than the villages and towns that surrounded her adoptive parents' farm. The past four days had been an incredible adventure in both passion and discovery, and it delighted him to share her joy.

Biryn sat on the soft, silvery sand of the beach, Cylena beside him, resting her head against his shoulder. They had one last evening of freedom before they had to return to

Cront. He had invited the two couples to eat with them and enjoy their last night of respite together. They sat around a campfire roasting fish the men had caught earlier in the evening.

Biryn toyed with a strand of Cylena's hair. "It has been a long time since I have escaped my duties, but tomorrow it is back to royal business."

Cylena kissed him on the cheek. "I have enjoyed this excursion very much. I will miss the walks along the shore and the beautiful sky when the suns set."

Biryn tightened his arm around her. "Then I will have to make it a point to bring you here often, my little songbird."

Erica nibbled on some fruit. "I am so thankful you invited us along, Biryn. Now I can say I've been on a real honeymoon. It's been loads of fun. I almost hate to go back, but I have missed our son."

Laro slipped his arm around Erica's shoulders. "I have missed Tomas, too."

Brenn took his fish off the spit and held it out to Ciara. "I am immensely grateful that it has been quiet. Aldis has reported no strange occurrences. It makes me dread what Zohmes and Odoxon may have plotted next."

Ciara scrunched up her face. "The quest to defeat Zohmes and Odoxon continues. We have had such a relaxing seven days, I did not want to bring the subject up, but I have spoken with Rania. The child Julia carries was sired by Zohmes when he was in possession of John's body."

Erica nodded. "After I heard what ailed her, that thought occurred to me. But the child would also be human, right? I shudder to think she's carrying Satan's baby."

"The infant has been infused with Zohmes' essence. That is all Rania could tell me."

Erica brushed her short curls out of her face, a troubled

expression clouding her face. "As I said, Satan's offspring. Julia doesn't remember what happened the evening of John's death. She doesn't know she had sex with the devil himself. It would destroy her."

"Satan?" Biryn queried.

"Like I explained when we were going to Yanata? Earth's equivalent of Zohmes."

Ciara set her plate on the sand. "Only we know. Remember I placed a spell on everyone else, so they would forget what they saw? We do not need to worry Julia or Laura."

"I agree. We will see how this develops. Meanwhile, let us enjoy what is left of our evening." Biryn took his datapad out of his pocket and turned on some soft music. Cylena hummed along with the music. He loved the sound of her melodious voice.

"This is heavenly. Tomorrow we go back to snow and cold." Erica shivered and snuggled against Laro.

Brenn's communicator sounded. He put it on speaker. "Aldis? What is wrong?"

"I hate to interrupt the last evening of your time away, but we have a crisis on our hands. I think it best you return to the palace immediately. I will have the team meet you there."

Brenn jumped up. "Crisis? Like what?"

"A sickness is spreading quickly among our people. Here is Catrice to explain it to you."

"Brenn, it's me." Catrice sounded agitated.

"Hello, Catrice. What is happening?"

"It's an epidemic and spreading fast. I have tested several people that have come down with the disease. It is called pneumonic plague on Earth. It is in the family of the bubonic plague. Erica will know about it. It is dangerous and deadly."

Biryn's heart sank. The last thing his people needed was an illness to sweep the planet. Cront had come a long way in rebuilding the city after the hurricane, but with many of the people still living in compounds, a communicable disease could overtake the city rapidly.

Brenn crossed his arms over his chest, concern in his voice. "How many ill so far?"

"We aren't sure. The bacteria is highly contagious and spread through contact from person to person via coughing or sneezing. It killed millions of people on Earth many centuries ago. Since then, it was almost eradicated on Earth. When we left, there were still a few reported cases."

"What are the symptoms?"

"Coughing, spitting up blood. Nausea and vomiting and a high fever. Headache, weakness, and bleeding under the skin. Unless a person is treated immediately, it is deadly."

Brenn paced back and forth in front of the fire, clearly agitated by what Catrice was telling them. "Do you have an antidote?"

"No. I have antibiotics, but there is no vaccine for this disease. At least, there wasn't when we left Earth."

"Could this have been carried to our planet from Earth?"

"Not unless one of the crew members was infected. All passed their physicals after they arrived here, and their bloodwork was fine."

Ciara came back to the campfire. Biryn had not even noticed that she'd left to seek some privacy.

"I just spoke with Rania. It appears that the last missing ships, your Initiation Four, and a cargo ship, carried what your people call germ warfare."

"You can't be serious." Catrice almost shouted it.

Erica stood and moved closer to the communicator and Brenn. "Catrice, the last ship that's missing had government officials and scientists aboard, and the last cargo vessel had a lot of their equipment on it and a load of medical supplies."

"Yes, I know."

Erica plopped to the sand. "Why would they have sent vials of germ warfare with us? It doesn't make sense."

"Maybe they sent it along as a type of defense against unfriendly aliens. God only knows what other viruses they've brought along. I seriously believe they also had an antidote, because releasing germ warfare would have affected our own people. I have to get back to work. The infected are almost beyond our capabilities to handle, and I don't know if we will have enough antibiotics. The sick continue to pour into the hospital. I have given the doctors at the hospital as much of the antibiotics as I can spare and have enlightened them about the virus. Many of the palace staff have the disease. There is a long line of people waiting near the infirmary. Jason and I, and the people in the main hospital lab, are working hard to duplicate what antibiotics we have with whatever we can find here on Ierilia. I'll see you all when you get back."

"Catrice, wait! Have there been any fatalities?" Biryn demanded to know.

"Yes. Three people have succumbed to the disease so far. I believe they may have been the first ones that were infected."

"Thank you." After Catrice disconnected, Biryn stood and faced Erica. "It was one of your ships that brought this epidemic upon us."

Erica's face twisted in shock. "Biryn, that's not fair. It's almost like you're accusing me. I had no idea of what was on the Initiation Four, and I believed the third cargo ship to carry only equipment and medical supplies. Can't Ciara use her tears to help the people that are ill?"

Biryn ran his hands through his hair. Deep down he knew Erica could not have known what exactly was on the last cargo ship, nor what her government may have planned for their destination planet. The woman had lost her own husband and child to sickness, due to the vaccination that was withheld from her family. "I apologize, Erica. I am deeply upset at what is happening to my people. No, there are limits as to what Ciara can do. As you saw when we rescued Cewrick, her tears could not heal him. This disease must be eradicated, or people will continue to fall ill. Ciara's tears may be able to heal, but they cannot always destroy a disease completely. We must leave, now, and return to the palace. Immediately."

Cylena placed her hand on his cheek. "Biryn, you need to calm. Let us pack up and return."

They hastily packed their gear, then headed for Biryn's flyer. The flight back to the palace would not take long. His thoughts were on what was happening to his people and how the Earth crews could have inflicted this upon them.

"Biryn, it was Zohmes and Odoxon. They have the last ship and the cargo ship in their possession somewhere. We need to find out where and retrieve those ships. Rania has sent my father to retrieve water from the Clyss. Though the water cannot cure this plague, its healing properties will help those that are stricken the most." Ciara patted him on the shoulder.

"Is this yet another test of my crown? What more are the gods and goddesses going to saddle me with?" Biryn cried out.

"It is not them that test you. It is Zohmes and Odoxon. Do not blame the ones that will guard you."

Tears soaked his cheeks. He felt totally powerless. He was supposed to have magick, yet what good would it do now? A hand rested on his forehead. Cylena's soft voice invaded his thoughts, calming him instantly.

Biryn placed his wineglass on the table and rubbed his forehead. The team had already been waiting for them in his quarters when they had returned from the Chircaul Coast. He should have known their seven-day reprieve from Zohmes and Odoxon was too good to be true. Like the hurricane, the ones to suffer for the latest atrocity were his people. Unlike the storm, this illness—or as Catrice called it, plague—could spread like dragon's fire across the planet, affecting many more people than just Cront and its outlying areas. "Why would Zohmes kill the very people he wishes to rule? I do not understand it."

Astiana's face was a mask of pain. "Zohmes does not care about the people of Ierilia. What matters to him is the hardship and strife he can cause, thus turning the people against you."

Cylena grasped his hand under the table. He gently squeezed her fingers. His little songbird had a spine of steel hidden beneath her quiet innocence. Her determination to help their people vibrated through him. Her magick swirled just below the surface, a living, breathing entity, and by the gods, she was powerful. "We will find a way to help our people."

The door burst open, startling them. Cewrick strode in, followed closely by Dunmore, who was making attempts to restrain him. Biryn held up his hand. "Let him speak, Dunmore. Cewrick? You look agitated. What is wrong?"

"Izarus spoke to me. I have to tell you where you can find the ships."

Icaras stood. "And we are supposed to believe you?"

Biryn slammed his fist on the table. "Silence, Icaras. How could he even know about the ships? Speak, Cewrick."

Cewrick ran his fingers through his hair. "I was asleep when Izarus woke me. The god told me you had returned to the palace and you were meeting with your team. The ships crashed on Feared Peaks. We must hasten to retrieve them and rescue the people from Earth out of Zohmes and Odoxon's clutches."

"We?" Icaras shouted.

"Yes. Izarus warned this would be a difficult mission and we will need all of our power. He ordered me to accompany you and help keep the king safe. We must all go. All four swords are necessary."

"This is a trap!" Icaras continued to shout. "You are in league with those two."

"Son, what can I do to convince you I am sincere?" Cewrick threw a helpless glance at Cylena.

Icaras stared at Cewrick, his body rigid with anger. "*You* are not my father, Cewrick. Do not call me your son again."

Ciara stood, pushing her chair back. "Icaras, I beg you to stop your verbal attack on your father. Rania just told me Cewrick is speaking the truth. Would the goddess lie to us?"

Icaras sank back to his chair, though he still scowled.

"Where is Feared Peaks?" Biryn asked. "I vaguely recall the name."

Aldis opened his datapad. A holograph appeared of the region. Biryn stared at the rugged terrain, jagged peaks rising from the ground, flanked and backed by snowy mountains. "Zoom in. What is that?"

"It looks like a man's face carved into the face of the tallest peak." Brenn leaned forward to examine the image closer.

"The peak is surrounded by a deep abyss. Look, there is a bridge leading into the mouth of that face. Can you zoom in even more, Aldis?" Laro asked.

"I see a strange green light coming from that opening." Cylena studied the image closer. "That is Zohmes' face. I clearly see the resemblance."

"As do I," Cewrick agreed.

"How could ships still be in one piece after crashing among

those peaks?" Erica shook her head disbelievingly.

Biryn cleared his throat. "Everyone, we can sit here and wonder, and stare at holographs, but that is not helping the matter. We need to get ready to leave. Aldis, how far is it?"

"Less than a day. We should try and rest for a few hours and leave at sunup."

"If we take a spaceship, we—" Biryn began.

"Impossible. You saw the terrain. We cannot land there. We will travel in the hovercraft, and even that cannot land close to the bridge. There is not enough room."

"I will tell the kitchen staff to get packs ready for all of us, in case it takes longer than a day. I will not be able to rest until we leave." Biryn stood and began to pace.

"I just had an epiphany," Erica said. "It takes two to seven days incubation period for the disease to take hold. We commented how quiet Zohmes and his ally have been these last seven days. I bet they released the virus on the day of your joining, or shortly after. They've been sitting back waiting for all this to happen."

"Erica, while we wait to leave, can you tell us more about this plague?" Ciara asked.

CHAPTER SEVENTEEN

Biryn was relieved when they were finally airborne. He was worried. If that cargo ship carried more vials of germ warfare, Zohmes could wipe out much of the population of Ierilia. Catrice would never have enough medicine. They had to stop them, fast, and retrieve the ships. Would any of the crew have survived? He was sure some had, because how would Zohmes have known about the germ warfare? It was an unknown phrase in their language, something none of their scientists had ever developed or would even consider creating. Deep down he prayed to the gods and goddesses that the ship had also carried medication and a possible vaccine. Catrice had told him there was no vaccine. But if the Earth scientists created the germ warfare virus, then surely they must have also had a vaccine? Maybe it had been kept secret.

Ciara turned to speak to them. "Rania told me what we saw on the face of that peak is one of Zohmes' temples where his priests live and his minions worship him."

"Maybe that's where they've stored the goods and medical equipment they've scavenged from the cargo ship." Erica twisted in her seat to face Ciara.

"And possible survivors?" Taylith added.

"Why couldn't you just zap us to the place?" Erica asked, raising her eyebrows. "It would be faster."

Laro chuckled. "And how would we transport survivors? That's if there are any. Our group is already large to zap as you call it."

"I cannot see a ship crashing on this dangerous terrain with so many sharp peaks and remain in one piece. I doubt there will be many survivors, but there must be some for Zohmes and Odoxon to have found out about the vials containing the virus." Astiana inserted her perspective.

"I agree with that," Cewrick mumbled.

"No one is interested in your opinion, Cewrick," Icaras snarled.

"Icaras, that is enough. We need you on these quests, but unless you keep a civil tongue, I will need to place a binding spell upon your lips." Ciara frowned angrily.

"Wow, I've never seen Ciara angry before," Erica said softly.

Biryn gave Icaras a hard look. "I agree with Ciara. This needs to stop, Icaras. Look out the window. We are closing in on Feared Peaks."

"I have actually found a spot to land. It is not far from the bridge," Aldis told them.

"That means the guards posted near the entrance will see us. Can you place a spell on them?" Biryn asked.

Astiana nodded. "We can and will. They will not see the ship or us crossing the bridge."

"I'm sure Zohmes and his buddy will know we're here," Erica said.

After Aldis landed the craft and opened the hatch, Biryn shivered. They all wore their skin suits, but the sudden gush of icy wind blowing inside was a shock to the face. He fastened the leather jacket he wore. Their gloves had the same effect as the skin suits. After he put them on, his hands warmed immediately.

They filed out of the craft onto the icy terrain. The piercing cold penetrated his boots, but the thermal socks ignited instantly, warming his feet. Thank the gods for the scientists who had invented the warming skin suits and other garments.

"Stay together. The bridge is not far from here," Brenn called out, his voice loud to make himself heard over the whistling wind.

Icaras glared at Cewrick and threw an elegantly carved, golden staff at him. A red jewel was embedded in the top, held by what appeared to be dragon's claws. "Here is your magick staff. I do not need or want it."

Cewrick caught the staff before it could hit the ground. "Thank you. This was a gift from Hirsuta when we joined."

Biryn sighed. His arm around Cylena's shoulders, he followed his warriors. "Stay close to me, love."

The bridge was narrow. They had to walk in twos. Biryn glanced beside him into the seemingly bottomless abyss and shuddered. They were almost midway when suddenly the bridge became a mass of flames. Cylena screamed. Biryn pulled her against him.

"Do not be afraid. It is an illusion!" Ciara yelled.

Continuing on through the flames, they reached the entrance. Zohmes or Odoxon must have alerted the guards and sent more because they faced at least ten creatures. Each appeared to have the body of a man, although quite grotesque. Hands that resembled claws held vicious-looking spears. The heads were a contortion of facial human tissue and bird. Large beaks protruded from where there should have been a mouth. Big protruding eyes bulged. The noses were merely two holes.

"Sexy dudes," Erica muttered as they stopped.

Laro, Ivran, and Brenn called out their lions. "They are magnificent," Cylena said close to Biryn's ear.

Biryn watched them, fascinated. The lions attacked, holding nothing back as they advanced on the guards. In a matter of minutes, the three lions had tossed the vermin into the abyss as if they were mere dolls.

They changed back, and Brenn turned to them with a big grin. "That was easy. Let us continue."

They walked through the entrance unhindered. The long, round passageway was illuminated in a green phosphorous glow, so they didn't need their glimmer sticks. The tunnel had tiny sparkling crystals embedded in the layers of ice. A chill ran down Biryn's spine as he looked at the skeletons trapped in the ice. Some were of humans, others of animals.

It was as if the passage wormed its way halfway into the ice mountain. A brighter green light gleamed at the end. Dripping water was all they heard. Thus far, nothing had attempted to stop them. He was wary and wondered what awaited them at the end. They stopped at the entrance to a huge cavern.

"We have reached the temple," Brenn announced. "I don't see anyone here."

They stepped through the opening and stood just inside the cavern. The ice formations were breathtaking as if carved by hand. Icicles hung from the ceiling, sparkling in the glow of the many sconces with torches placed strategically on the walls. The torches burned steadily, the flames not orange but a bright red that sent a creepy glow throughout, reflecting on the icicles above.

They began to move forward. "There have to be more chambers," Aldis commented. "I cannot believe there is nothing here."

A loud rumbling echoed through the cavern. Biryn swiveled. "The tunnel is blocked!"

"Illusion?" Taylith wondered.

"No, not this one." Astiana laughed. "They are trying to trap us."

"No one can trap us here. Not with so many sorcerers present," Cewrick hissed.

Ciara nodded. "Exactly. They are underestimating us. Zohmes and Odoxon have no idea that your powers are back."

A growl echoed through the chamber, followed by more. The team stood close together in a tight ring, back to back, protecting each other.

Large creatures covered in long, white hair moved from the shadows. They had tiny red eyes. Long snouts with two fangs protruding from a small mouth. Their ears were tall and curved. They closed in on the group.

Biryn grasped Cylena's hand, keeping her near to him. "What are those?"

"They look kind of like polar bears, only much bigger, and their heads are weird," Erica said.

"They are an unknown species. I suspect they are a Zohmes creation," Brenn told them.

"The way they are circling and inspecting us, it looks as if they want us for their next meal," Taylith said.

"I am not prepared to just stand here and wait for an attack," Cewrick mumbled and instantly began to softly chant a spell. A breeze kicked up around them, gaining in strength. A burst of light illuminated the cavern, engulfing the furred monsters, disintegrating them as the light receded.

"Well, he didn't even give us time to get cuddly with the teddy bears." Erica sounded amazed.

"Teddy bear?" Biryn shook his head. Why would anyone

want to get cuddly with the vermin? He was as shocked as Erica at how quickly Cewrick had handled the monsters. Cewrick made using his magick look so easy. Even Icaras and Ciara had to concentrate when using their powers, although Ciara and Icaras were centuries younger than the sorcerer and neither experienced as of yet, especially Icaras. Both their powers had been bound while Cewrick had been possessed by Zohmes.

Ciara giggled. "Brenn is wondering the same."

"Ummm...a child's toy. Sweet, huggable, snuggly...kind of like Laro." Erica grinned at her mate.

Sweet? Huggable? Snuggly? Biryn grimaced. Women said all manner of nonsense about their mates. He was not saying another word lest Cylena join in.

The glow of the ice walls drew his attention. The torches' flames danced across the floor, leading his gaze to an altar of carved ice. Garish faces and ghouls were etched into the pillars, and bones of humans and other creatures were scattered along the top. Candles in carved sconces stood on each corner, casting an eerie light. Behind the altar, the ice concentrated into an almost mirror-like surface. Translucent and thick, it began to glow with a red fierce blaze of light. Ten priests dressed in black robes edged in gold, a strange design embroidered onto the front of the robes, stepped through the wall of ice to stand behind the altar. Their silver hair was swept up into a cone shape on top of their heads. Anger contorted their angular faces. One stepped forward and started lighting incense, pouring an oil within the skulls on the altar. Thin tendrils of a greenish smoke drifted up and outward. A strange scent permeated the air.

Biryn stepped in front of Cylena. "I think we have a serious problem."

A chant reverberated around them. The low murmur built

into a crescendo as bodies took shape from thin air. The priests appeared to glide through the mirror-like wall behind the altar, vanishing from view. Within moments of their disappearance, hundreds of Zohmes' minions materialized in the cavern, clad in black cloaks and wielding ensorcelled swords. One last figure, larger than the others, appeared before them. His aged face was a mask of fury. In his hand he held a black staff, the crystal on top glowing a bright green as he worked his magick.

"Odoxon!" Cewrick grasped his staff and pointed it at the sorcerer, the murmur of a spell leaving his lips.

Biryn pulled his sword, and he noticed Taylith, Brenn, and Erica had drawn theirs as well. "Stay close to me, songbird. I will not chance you getting hurt."

As soon as the two sorcerers locked in battle, the minions swarmed the rest of them like vermin stalking their prey. Biryn swung at the creatures, attempting to keep them at bay. Beside him Cylena chanted a spell, joining Icaras, Ciara, and Astiana throwing ropes of fire toward the cloaked figures. Roars reverberated around him when Brenn, Ivran, and Laro shifted, the lions ripping a path through the sea of bodies.

The battle seemed endless. With each minion Biryn killed, it seemed two took its place. The altar caught his eye. The mirror of ice behind it shifted and moved, the glow brightening, a face taking shape. Flaming hair, a mask of hatred, and eyes that stared right through him.

Zohmes.

Zohmes joined in the chanting of Odoxon's spell, strengthening it. The minions had them cornered. There was no way to coordinate their attack or join their use of magick. With Zohmes in the mix, the horde was almost undefeatable. A whirlwind kicked up of black smoke and flame, streaming through the cavern, surrounding the team in its tendrils.

Wind blasted around them, and Biryn felt as if he were falling into a chasm. He tried to grab Cylena's hand, but the force of the wind whisked her away from him.

Total blackness. No sounds. Everyone was gone.

"Cylena!" He shouted her name but heard no answer. His stomach rolled. The spinning sensation became faster.

Suddenly his feet hit solid substance. The spiraling slowed, and the blackness receded. Cylena's hand grasped his so hard, the blood stopped flowing. He pulled her into his arms as the air cleared around him. They were all there, the whole team, but where in the gods were they?

"We're in an ice dungeon," Erica muttered.

Biryn's eyes adjusted to the dim light. "It appears so. We are not the only ones here. Look in the far corner."

They turned. A group of people huddled together looked at them with fear.

"It's the crew from the Initiation Four." Erica hurried toward them. Taking her glimmer stick out of her belt, she held it up. "Caroline, Lucy, Chloe, are all of you here? Did the whole crew make it?"

"Oh my God. It's Erica!" A man stepped toward her.

"It's the captain! Ethan, did everyone survive?"

"Yes, but we're not all here. Dr. Reed, Dr. Brooks, and Barry Sullivan, the president's chief of staff, are in league with the crazy guys that rescued us." Ethan scowled and gestured to the ice wall. "The only way we're allowed out of here is if we join with them to fight the aliens on the surface."

"Fantastic. Well, some of those aliens are standing right here with me to rescue you." She quickly introduced each of the team, last of all Biryn.

"A king? That's awesome. Where are we?" Caroline asked.

"The planet is called Ierilia. One of those crazies wants to overthrow the king and rule the planet. That's it in short. We need to get out of here."

A rumbling caused her to step back toward the team. "What is that?"

Biryn looked at the wall. A block of ice moved, displaying an opening just wide enough for someone to step through.

"Captain Erica Martinez. What a pleasant surprise finding you here, accompanied by the aliens."

Barry Sullivan, former chief of staff to the president, walked toward her. The two scientists were close on his heels. Behind them stood Odoxon.

"Are you out of your fucking mind giving those bastards germ warfare?" Erica almost shouted the words.

Barry sneered at them. "Of course I told them what we had and gave it to them. In order to defeat the aliens and for us to live on the surface, we have to help them."

Erica shook her head. "You're out of your mind. They've brainwashed the three of you. They're very good at that. You do realize you're dealing with an angry fallen god and an ancient sorcerer?"

Dr. Reed stepped toward her. "We are quite fascinated by the abilities that exist on this planet."

Dr. Brooks joined him. "Yes. Odoxon has informed us that we now have everyone we need in custody necessary for our experiments."

Erica burst out laughing. "You three have no clue who and what you are dealing with. Odoxon is pure evil. You can't trust him for a nanosecond."

Odoxon joined the conversation. "Pretty lady, we really have little use for you or the others from the ship except for us to use for our experimentations." He told the two scientists and Barry, "I will leave the three of you with the prisoners to convince them. Although there are other ways, I prefer to have them assist us willingly, so we will give you time with them." Odoxon left the dungeon. The block of ice slid back into place.

Erica turned to the team. "You all had your translators on? You heard?"

"Yes. We did. Ask them where the cargo is, Erica," Biryn told her.

She turned to face the three men. "Where is the cargo from the cargo ship? How much of it was saved?"

"All of it," Chloe answered. "Those dudes saw the ships coming and stopped them from crashing onto the peaks. Then they brought us all out of stasis, and we woke up here. I presume they transported the cargo the same way."

"Where are they keeping it?"

"In the next room."

"Room? Haha. That's funny." Erica turned to Aldis. "We'll need a cargo ship to take it all out of here. It won't fit in the hovercraft."

"My communicator doesn't work here. How will we do that? We need one of our space cargo ships," Aldis answered.

Astiana spoke. "Leave it to Ciara, Rania, and me. We will get the request through to Dunmore."

"You speak their language," Barry said. "What did you just tell them and what did they say?"

"Just translating." She turned to Biryn. "We need to get out of here fast before those crazy power hungry idiots want to begin their experiments."

Swiveling, she asked the scientists, "So you two have a lab all set up?"

"No. Not yet. Odoxon is planning on taking us all and our equipment to his castle on the surface now that you're all here. His plan worked brilliantly. Even the king joined in the rescue." Dr. Brooks snickered.

Biryn cleared his throat. "We need to get out of here fast.

Before Odoxon puts his plan into action."

"I suggest we bind these three first. I will attend to that now." Cewrick mumbled some strange words, held out his staff, and glowing red rings bound the three men from shoulders to ankles. "I have also silenced them."

"Good. I don't want to hear any more of their crap!" Erica spat the words out.

"How can we get into the next room?" Biryn wondered aloud.

Biryn noticed the two scientists' eyes almost popped out of their heads when Cewrick pointed his staff at the wall and melted a big hole in the ice. Biryn stepped through the hole and looked at the many crates stacked almost to the ceiling.

"Icaras, Cylena, Ciara, Astiana, and Biryn. We need to combine our magick to transport these goods to the surface all at once when the ship lands. The same with all the people here. We can do it. We will send everyone directly into the hovercraft so we can take off immediately," Cewrick told them.

Biryn was pleased that Icaras did not argue with Cewrick. "That is a lot of people to get up there at once. Eleven of us, and thirty-two Earth people. Will the magick shackles hold during transport? When we get the three prisoners back to the palace, they will go to the dungeons for now until we can question them further."

"Rania just contacted me," Ciara told them. "The space cargo ship has been dispatched and should arrive soon. Let us begin the transport before Odoxon and Zohmes discover what we are up to."

"Erica, tell your people to stand very close in a group while we attend to the cargo," Cewrick commanded.

"Everyone, come and stand in the center and huddle as close to each other as you can. We are getting out of here,"

Erica informed the crew.

"How?" Ethan asked.

"No time for explanations. Just do it."

"Rania just informed me that the spaceship has landed next to the hovercraft." The six sorcerers stepped through the hole and, holding hands, began to chant. A vivid blue swirling light lit up the icy chamber. Within seconds, all the cargo had disappeared.

"Now all of us and the crew," Ciara mumbled.

Biryn knew using so much magick had to be draining. The six stood very close to the group huddling together and chanted again. He held tightly on to Cylena, his hand behind her head. The blue light almost blinded him, so he closed his eyes.

When he opened them, they stood inside the hovercraft. Looking out the window, he saw the cargo ship taking off.

"Strap in, everybody," Aldis called out while he ignited the engines. "Some of you will need to secure the prisoners."

CHAPTER EIGHTEEN

Biryn had never been so glad to be back in his chambers. The crew had already been taken to the compound and the three prisoners secured in the dungeons. The team all sat around his table while waiting for dinner, sipping a glass of eldalas spirit. Even Cylena drank hers, although he knew she didn't really like it.

"A toast to a successful mission!" He held up his glass.

They toasted, and the men emptied their glasses. Dunmore quickly refilled them. "It went a lot faster than I thought it would." Brenn drank a bit from his second drink. "Let me thank and toast Cewrick. Without him, I think we would have encountered a lot more problems."

Cewrick held his glass up. "A toast to the gods and goddesses who gave me back all my powers. And to my children, who promise to become just as powerful, if not more, than me."

Icaras took a sip from his glass. "We survived this long without your help. I have no doubt we would have survived this mission without you."

Cylena gave her brother a pained look. "Icaras, please. We have enough to deal with. Do not add to the problems we face."

Cylena entwined her fingers with Biryn's. "I had no doubt we would find a way to help our people." She released his hand, stood, and walked around the table to Icaras. She grasped his hands and pulled him to his feet. "Icaras, I love you, and I know you are hurting, but you have blinded yourself to our father's pain and refuse to see his innocence. To heal, you must forgive, and to forgive, you must open yourself up to his wounds. We need to work together if we are to save our mother."

Biryn felt her power surge along their bond. Her love for both her brother and her father burned brightly. She caressed Icaras' cheek, her stormy eyes glowing. Icaras gasped, his hands clenched at his sides. Biryn knew what Icaras was feeling—that gentle power of hers edging its way inside, sinking deep within and wrapping itself around your soul, connecting the bonds of son to father. Icaras could have blocked her, shut her out and bound their connection just as he did Cewrick's, but Biryn knew he wouldn't. Icaras loved his sister too much to ever hurt her in such a way.

Tears streamed down Icaras' face as he hugged Cylena and kissed her cheek. "I will try, sister. For you, I will try to forgive him."

Cylena and Icaras returned to their seats, Icaras pouring himself another glass of eldalas and downing it.

Biryn glanced at Cewrick. He looked as if he would be sick. Cylena had opened a floodgate between father and son. Cewrick had to know without a doubt how Icaras felt. The wounds that had been driven into a young boy's soul perpetrated by the only father he'd ever known were still raw. By the gods, he hoped they both could move past the pain and betrayal. The path to forgiveness and healing was long, but with Cylena's love and generous heart helping them, maybe

Icaras could forgive his father.

Catrice hailed Biryn on his communicator, interrupting his thoughts. "Yes, Catrice?"

"We found plenty of antibiotics, and there is also a vaccine. Those bastards created the vaccine years ago, but it was never released."

"How many fatalities are there now?"

"Fourteen. Now that we have the vaccine, there is enough to inoculate thousands, and we have more than enough antibiotics. We'll get on top of the pandemic."

Biryn sighed in relief. Thank the gods there was a vaccine on board the cargo ship. Now his people stood a chance against this plague. "Fantastic. Please update me regularly?"

"Jason is on his way to your chambers with a vial of the vaccine to administer inoculations to you and your team."

"Thank you, Catrice." Biryn closed his communicator and set it on the table.

Erica tapped her fingers. "Biryn, the people that died from the illness need to be cremated."

"Cremated?"

Erica brushed a stray curl out of her face. "Burned or incinerated…to kill the bacteria. It is the same pathogen that causes the bubonic plague, and I am not sure what animals or insects you may have on Ierilia that can harbor disease."

"Dunmore, see that Catrice has the assistance she needs to handle the incineration of the bodies. I have no wish for the bacteria to thrive and spread."

"Of course, Sire."

A knock sounded at the door. Dunmore hurried to open it, letting Jason inside the chambers. "Your Majesty, I hate to interrupt, but I need to administer the vaccines."

Biryn lounged on his bed, Cylena nestled in his arms, a

strand of her silky hair wrapped around his finger. The team had left not long after Jason had given everyone a shot of the vaccine, and he looked forward to spending some time alone with his mate, even if it was for a short period of rest. If he could even rest. Thoughts of the plague—and Icaras—still worried him. He knew the gods had given them the gift of the vaccine, but there was no god or goddess that could repair the rift between Icaras and Cewrick. "Do you think Icaras can forgive your father? He was just a boy when he was banished. All he ever knew was a man who was not really his father. It was Zohmes."

"It will take time, but I know he will." She ran her fingers across his chest, up his neck, and to his jaw. "Right now, I do not want to think about anything but us."

He caressed her cheek, then kissed her, lightly nipping her bottom lip with his teeth. She giggled and lightly bit his lip back, the sharp pleasure of it shooting straight to his cock. Catching her by the waist, he eased her over his body to straddle his hips. Her long raven hair spilled over her shoulders in unruly curls. He reached up, teasing the pert nipple peeking through the silky strands, then caressed the underside of her breast, filling his hand with its firm softness. Her body arched, the velvety wetness of her core brushing his throbbing cock, making him ache to take her. He released her breast and pulled her down, taking one nipple, then the other into his mouth, tormenting them until her throaty moans of pleasure permeated the air around him.

Cylena grasped him by the hair, pulling him from her breast, and kissed him hungrily. "I need you *now*, Biryn."

She reached between their bodies, grasped his cock, and guided it to her slick opening, impaling herself on the hard length of him. Gods, she took his breath away. She threw her head back in wild abandon, her ivory skin gleaming in the moonlight filtering through the windows. Growling her name, he gripped her hips, driving into her with each thrust of her hips. Her body spasmed around him, her orgasm rippling through her, pulling him along over the edge into the chasm of ecstasy.

Biryn turned to his side, settling Cylena beside him, and kissed the top of her head. "I love you, my songbird."

She giggled, kissed his chest, and snuggled close to him. "I love you, too, my sweet teddy bear."

Morning came all too soon. Cylena had rolled away from him while she slept and lay so still, he had to look closely to see if she was breathing. A small smile played on her lips, and he wondered what she was dreaming. He sighed. It was going to be a busy day – the prisoners from the Earth ship to deal with, the plague, and other pressing court matters.

He got out of bed, being careful not to disturb her, and hastened to bathe and dress. After he was done, he checked on Cylena one more time and smiled as he saw her still sleeping peacefully.

The hearing would be private. He did not wish his court to turn against the people from Earth. Only his team were to be present for it. He had invited them to have breakfast with him, so they were already waiting for him in his dining room, sitting around the table.

"Morning, everyone." He motioned to Dunmore that they were ready for breakfast.

"Sire, the queen – "

"Is still fast asleep. I will let her rest a little while longer."

Dunmore hurried away to alert the kitchen staff to serve breakfast.

"Brenn, Laro, and Ivran, after we eat, you will fetch the prisoners from the dungeons and take them to my private office. We need to deal with this matter privately."

"Biryn, they caused the deaths of fourteen of our people. Shouldn't they be put on trial?" Aldis asked.

"They caused those deaths inadvertently. It is Zohmes and Odoxon that should be standing trial for multiple murder. The three Earthlings were deceived by them into thinking there were unfriendly aliens on the surface. We will question them, talk to them."

A string of servants entered carrying platters of food. They set them on the table, filled everyone's glasses with jago milk, and left the room.

They had barely begun eating when Cylena joined them. "My queen," Biryn said, standing up and pulling her chair out for her.

"You could have woken me," Cylena scolded.

He smiled and kissed her hand. "You looked too peaceful and seemed to be enjoying a nice dream."

"Is Cewrick going to partake in everything now?" Icaras asked, a frown on his forehead.

Cylena gave Icaras a pointed look. "Brother, our father is on our side. Until Zohmes and Odoxon are defeated and banished for all eternity, his aid will be invaluable to us. Learn to accept what has been written, or the gods and goddesses will frown upon you."

Biryn nodded. "Cewrick belongs to our team now. As your and your sister's father, he is also family."

Biryn sighed. He fully understood Icaras' reluctance to accept Cewrick. Dunmore approached, handing Biryn his communicator. "Yes, Catrice."

"Your Majesty—"

"Biryn to you. I will not tell you again."

"Sorry. I am happy to report that we're beating the plague. We worked through the night to inoculate the healthy and administer antibiotics to the ill. Today, there have been no new cases reported from the hospital or here at the palace."

"Good work, Catrice."

"We've also gone through the cargo and discovered a lot more germ warfare vials and cylinders containing nerve gas. Jason and I have destroyed them all."

"That is good news. What about the deceased? Has that been taken care of?"

"Almost. We have spoken with the family members and explained what needed to be done. They understand but asked for a mass departure to the realm of dreams ceremony. We told them we would speak to you. How do we proceed?"

"I will instruct the building of a raft large enough to hold all fourteen deceased. The families will know how to proceed from there, but the bodies have to be handled with care."

"A raft?"

"When a member of the general population enters the realm of dreams, the family holds a ceremony on the beach, or a riverbank, or a lake, whichever is in their vicinity. The deceased is placed on a raft piled high with wood from the snya tree. The body is placed on top, usually dressed in their finest clothing."

"Biryn, the families can't touch the bodies or even get close."

"You have told them this?"

"Yes. They did not like it. The bodies will be contained in zakuna bags. The doctors at the hospital told me these bags will protect the contaminated tissues from possibly infecting healthy people."

"It cannot be helped. The raft is usually heavily decorated with flowers. It is winter now, so they will use branches from various everlasting trees. Each member of the family will place a departure gift on the raft. A ceremony takes place while the raft is pushed out onto the water. Once it is in the sea, river, or lake, our archers will shoot lit torches to set it on fire. The ceremony continues and then the family feasts to celebrate their deceased family member entering the realm of dreams."

"Wow, that is similar to how the Vikings used to do it," Erica exclaimed.

"Vikings?" Biryn raised his eyebrows.

"Ancient Earth history. Many centuries ago there were a people called Vikings. Their realm of dreams was called Valhalla."

"Erica, I'm far too busy to listen to our history. I'll keep you informed, Biryn." Catrice signed off.

"I am glad Catrice managed to deal with the situation." Biryn resumed eating.

"I would like to learn more about Hirsuta. Ciara or Astiana, can you speak with Rania about my mother?" Icaras looked at them both.

"It is a hypothesis suggested by Cylena based on her own experience and Cewrick's description of what happened to her. I have mentioned it to Rania, but we have been far too busy with other matters. If the book of knowledge decrees it, we will learn the truth, but only when we are allowed to know," Astiana answered.

Ciara placed her fork and knife on her plate and looked at Icaras. "I wouldn't get my hopes up too much. Even if it sounds similar to Cylena's disappearance, Zohmes might not have used the same spell."

"What I wonder is why is all this happening now? Why is Zohmes pushing so hard for the throne after so many centuries?" Erica joined the conversation.

"Zohmes has spent those centuries plotting the demise of the royal line. Like a game of battle theft, he put his minions into place, patiently waiting for his strategy to work. And it was working. As written in the book of knowledge, when Brenn entered the pool in the Clyss, he set all of this in motion. Ciara gave him her soul shard, allowing him to release her from captivity. If he had not waded into that water, and Ciara was still bound to the pool, all would still be as before. Zohmes' plan would still be in motion, but we would not have the power to stop him," Astiana told her.

Biryn cringed. What a sobering thought. The book of knowledge contained many possible futures. One wrong choice and the outcome could be very dire indeed. "If everyone has finished, it is time for the hearing." He stood and held out his hand to Cylena. "Please bring the prisoners to my office?" he directed at Brenn, Ivran, and Laro.

CHAPTER NINETEEN

There weren't enough chairs in Biryn's office for them all to sit. Biryn sat behind his desk. Cylena stood next to him. The other men stood and allowed the women the remaining chairs. They didn't have to wait long before the door opened, and the prisoners were led in by the three men.

Brenn, Ivran, and Laro joined the team and stood behind Biryn while the prisoners stood before the large desk.

"Aldis, you may begin," Biryn ordered.

Aldis attached a translator to the men's uniforms, then picked up his datapad and began questioning the prisoners. "Please state your name and age."

"Barry Sullivan, former chief of staff to the president of the United States of America, thirty-eight."

"Dr. Jacob Reed, medical research scientist, thirty-four."

"Dr. Thaddeus Brooks, biological scientist, twenty-nine."

Aldis swiped the screen of the datapad and glanced up at the prisoners. "The first charge against each of you is murder. Fourteen of our people suffered a terrible death because of your alliance with the enemy. The second charge is aiding and abetting the enemy. How do you plead?"

"Not guilty." The three spoke in unison.

Biryn studied the three men. Sullivan was short in stature, slightly balding, and almost came across as frail. He wore some kind of goggles over his brown eyes. He made a mental note to ask Erica about them. Jacob Reed was also short, slim, with black hair, slanted eyes, and yellowish skin. He looked different from the other Earth people. Brooks was taller, with blue eyes, brown hair, and a bearded face.

Aldis placed the datapad on Biryn's desk and crossed his arms over his chest. "What possessed you to bring chemical warfare along on your journey?"

Barry Sullivan answered. "Our president ordered us to do so in case of unfriendly aliens. We believed the destination planet to be unpopulated, but just in case we came across alien beings or monsters we could not fight with normal weapons, we could unleash a virus or nerve gas. We are only two hundred and twenty-four."

"Were. Not all of our people survived," Erica interrupted.

Aldis continued. "At the risk of exposing yourselves and the others to terrible diseases?"

Barry shifted on his feet. "We were all inoculated against infection."

"Were all the people on all of the ships inoculated? When Zohmes and Odoxon released you from stasis, what did they tell you?"

"That they are the master race but had been driven to live underground by the aliens on the surface."

Biryn snickered. "Master race indeed."

Barry frowned. "How were we supposed to know? We crashed on an alien planet, and the first people we met were the two men that call themselves Zohmes and Odoxon. What they told us was very believable. But you all look like normal humans. They don't, and neither do the beings that serve them. As for your earlier question, I don't know if all the members of the expedition were inoculated. I just know we were."

"Most of the people of Ierilia appear like us, though there are some inhabitants in various realms that look different. Ierilia is a planet created by the gods and goddesses. It has been in existence for many centuries, more than you can imagine. They created us, but there are also a few species from different planets that we have given sanctuary to. The Ierilians are a peaceful people," Brenn told them.

Aldis picked his datapad up and brought up a holograph of their excursion into Odoxon's castle. After it finished playing, he showed another of their quest into Yanata to rescue Cylena.

"Oh my God. Those are the people from the Initiation Three," Jacob shouted.

"Exactly. Zohmes and Odoxon had them imprisoned, with the queen, in Yanata," Aldis explained.

Erica spoke up. "Yanata being their version of Hell. We had quite a time rescuing everyone."

Barry gave Erica a quizzical look. "Erica, it sounds like you trust these people a hundred percent."

She squared her shoulders and gave the three prisoners a pointed stare. "I do. Our ship was the first they found. I've been here for quite a while and have learned their language and their customs. Ierilia is truly a magical planet. If only Zohmes and Odoxon would leave it alone."

"I genuinely regret now ever having told them about and giving them the vials of germ warfare. We only gave them one kind. There were other variations." Thaddeus looked truly repentant.

"Whatever was left in the cargo has been destroyed," Biryn said.

Jacob looked startled. "Everything?"

"The germ warfare vials and the nerve gas cylinders. All the equipment is in our science facility, and all medications and hospital supplies are with the doctor," Ivran informed him.

Biryn was deep in thought. What was he to do with these individuals from Earth? Zohmes and Odoxon had misled them. If they would have known the truth, would these men have given up the secret of the germ warfare vials? They had not deliberately committed murder. Zohmes and his ally had committed the crimes.

"What about our equipment? Will you return it to us, or are you keeping it?" Thaddeus demanded to know.

"For now. After our own scientists inspect it and our engineers adjust it to Ierilian technology, it will be released," Aldis reassured him.

Biryn stood. "I have another question. You were unaware of the nature of the two that saved your ships and released you from stasis. You believed what they told you. Yet they kept your crew imprisoned. Why?"

"The crew did not agree with us handing over the germ warfare so readily. It caused discord between us. So, Zohmes and Odoxon decided to keep them in the dungeons until they changed their minds," Brooks answered.

"Did you not find it strange that your crew would not follow your example?" Ivran asked.

Barry adjusted his glasses. "Yes, and no. We thought it was because of the effects of being in stasis for a long period and the crash. I'm sorry. We are deeply at fault here."

"When they took us into custody, you mentioned that you had everyone you needed to start your experiments. What experiments were you referring to?" Taylith asked in a hard tone.

Jacob pinched the bridge of his nose. "Zohmes and Odoxon

said their people were dying. They wanted us to find a way to help them find a cure." He gestured to Biryn and the rest of the team. "Zohmes said the key to saving their people was in your DNA. That must have been a lie as well."

Biryn felt a mind brush his and heard a whisper in Taylith's voice. *He could be telling the truth. Zohmes did many experiments while in Cewrick's body. He wished to create an army of indestructible beings by harnessing the strengths of many of Ierilia's races. Remember his minions that attacked and captured us? Their deformed faces? They were some of his creations. I do not know if he was successful with his other experiments besides the urcals.* Thankful for the insight, Biryn filed the information away for future investigation. If Zohmes had managed to create a large army of his hybrids, they might not stand a chance in defeating him.

Biryn ran a hand through his hair. "At this time, I am unsure what to do with you. Do we put you on trial for murder? I do not think that is fair, as it was Zohmes and Odoxon that committed the crime. We have given the people from Earth a realm of their own and will help them to build. The numbers are not completely correct, as some perished. The survivors have been given the chance to build a new community on my planet. They can use the help of the last survivors from Earth. Let me ask you. Do you believe now that we are not the aliens you were made to imagine?"

"No. Nothing is as it was told to us," Jacob answered.

"Correct. Therefore, I am going to release you, on the condition that you integrate with the other people from Earth. Just like the other survivors, you will live in a compound where you will learn our language and study our history. Once all Earth people have graduated from the compound, we will help build your first city. We are prepared to supply the means, the materials, and everything you need. All we want is for you to be happy on our planet and live according to our laws and under my rule."

"Phew, that is a relief." Erica spoke softly, but loud enough for Biryn to hear.

He looked at her while powering off his translator. "What did you expect, Erica?"

"I thought you'd send them through the trial by fire."

Biryn kept his voice low. "No. Your fellow travelers were not the murderers. Zohmes and Odoxon were. Your Earth people were duped into believing them."

"So you're letting them off?"

"If you mean I am not punishing them, yes. It was not of their doing. As I said, Zohmes and Odoxon were behind everything. I will allow your people freedom to settle on Ierilia, providing they respect our customs and laws." He jabbed at the on button on his translator and turned his head to face the three prisoners.

"I apologize for the interruption. Erica had some questions for me. Aldis?"

Aldis stepped forward again. "King Biryn has been lenient. I will have you transported to the compound. Do you have any questions?"

"We are grateful for the king's leniency. Yes, we have many questions." Barry looked at Erica. "Can you meet with us later?"

Erica nodded. "I'll see if I can go to the compound this afternoon."

Dunmore escorted them out of the office. "Let us go to my quarters for some refreshments," Biryn suggested.

While they were discussing recent events and enjoying coffee and tea with some delicious cookies and cake, Laro's communicator beeped. "My parents. They are at Xynnar overseeing the rebuilding." He turned the speaker on.

"Laro here."

"Son, you need to contact the king." Laro's father sounded agitated.

"What is wrong?"

"All the forever trees around Xynnar and the surrounding valley are turning black and twisted, their leaves a dark blood red. Also on the mountains, as far as we can see, the forests and vegetation are thinning. Our vegetable and fruit crops in the hothouses are wilting and seem to be dying."

"A disease? Contaminated soil caused by the Toubosian attack, maybe?"

"If it was caused by the attack, it would have appeared long ago and affected our regular crops."

"True. I have you on speaker. We are with King Biryn at the moment, so he knows of the situation. I will talk to you later." He clicked off and looked at the team. "You heard."

"Another Zohmes trick?" Erica sipped from her coffee.

Biryn frowned. "We need to find out if this is global. Contact our botanists and see if there are other reports."

Ciara tapped her fingers on the table. "I have an answer for this. Niqine and the handmaidens need to return to their natural habitat, the Xynnar mountains. It is because of their long absence that the vegetation is beginning to die."

Biryn looked at her quizzically. "They have been gone from there for centuries. Why is this happening now?"

"The region is unprotected. Zohmes and Odoxon could have interfered with the soil. The absence of the little people also caused the koriam crystals and ore to become unstable, which has been a problem for quite some time."

"Niqine is on the Tideless Abyss. Only Ciara and I can go there to bring her and the handmaidens home to the Xynnar Valley," Taylith informed them.

Erica set her mug on the table. "Laura is our botanist. She also studied dendrology. Why not let her examine the plants, soil, and trees first?"

"I can go and get Laura and fly her there," Taylith offered.

"If this is interference through magick, what good can that do?" Biryn asked.

"Biryn, I am not sure if Zohmes and Odoxon are behind this. I have not spoken with Rania. It could very well be that it is because Niqine and her people are missing from the Xynnar Valley. Or it could be some sort of natural disease. It is a good idea to have Laura investigate first," Ciara told him.

"Yes, before we jump to conclusions. Allowing Laura to do this will stop the information from leaking to the population and causing panic," Brenn agreed.

"Sire, if I may speak?" Dunmore queried.

Biryn nodded. "What is it, Dunmore?"

"I discreetly contacted the science facility and asked if there have been any reports of late without mentioning what is happening in Xynnar. They said there were none."

Biryn rubbed his chin. "Ciara could be right in that it is finally happening because of Niqine's absence or a natural plant disease. We will wait for Laura's report first." Biryn turned to Cewrick. "From her reaction at the joining celebration, I do not believe that Laura realizes who you are. She and her colleague, Mark, suffered greatly at your hands while Zohmes possessed you. Do not draw attention to yourself while she is here."

A pained expression twisted Cewrick's face. "I was shown what Zohmes had done to them. Maybe it is best for now that she not be told who I am."

"Laura is much stronger than any of you realize, and I will not hide the truth from her. We have kept enough secrets from her already." Taylith drew Biryn's attention.

"I agree with Taylith. We can't hide this from her. It will only make matters worse, and depending on her test results, she may have to work closely with us to find out what is happening," Erica pointed out.

CHAPTER TWENTY

L unch had just been served, and the servants were leaving Biryn's quarters when Taylith returned, accompanied by Laura. Her gaze traveled the room, then landed on Cewrick. She squared her shoulders and raised her chin, a defiant look in her eyes. She was no longer the frightened young woman Biryn had met after her rescue from Cewrick's clutches. She stood before them, confident, without fear. The only telltale sign of her upset was the death grip she had on Taylith's arm. He moved closer to her and whispered something. Her attention diverted to him, she nodded, then released his arm to pull her datapad from her bag.

"That was fast," Biryn commented. "Would you like to join us for lunch? Laura, you, too, but tell us about your test results first?"

Laura swiped her fingers across the screen of her datapad and handed it to Biryn. "Your Majesty, I took my kit with me and tested soil samples from the greenhouses, the forest, and the mountains. I conducted tests for known Earth and Ierilian plant diseases and infestations as well as contaminants that could be affecting the soil. As you can see from the test results, all came back normal. I could find nothing in the soil or vegetation. I also saw no sign of the disease in the forests and vegetation beyond the Xynnar region."

"Thank you, Laura." Biryn handed the datapad back to her. She returned it to her bag and allowed Taylith to lead her to a chair at the table.

"Ciara and Taylith, please go to the Tideless Abyss to bring Niqine and the handmaidens home, but I want you to take us with you. Our flyers cannot go there, or our hovercrafts. The thought has crossed my mind that this could be a Zohmes and Odoxon trap. We shall depart after lunch."

Erica cleared her throat. "Is it far? I told Barry I would visit the compound this afternoon."

Biryn glanced at Erica. "Why do you need to visit him? There are people assigned to the compound that can answer his questions."

Erica scrunched up her nose. "I think Barry is still in his chief of staff mode. He worked directly with our president, and the government designated him as the leader of our group of ships and all our people. I am guessing that he believes that because I am part of your team and work closely with you, that I am now some kind of head honcho."

"Honcho? Your Earth words do not make any sense."

Erica grinned at Biryn. "They make perfect sense to me. Honcho or *head* honcho is the person in charge. Like a ruler."

"At least that one didn't include huggable or cuddly." Biryn took a drink of his wine. "The Tideless Abyss is not far with the dragons taking us there."

"Didn't someone say it was located somewhere behind unscalable mountains?" Erica helped herself to meat, cheese, and bread.

Ciara brushed her hair out of her face. "There are many warped tales about the realm and where it is. No one can go there. No flyers, spaceships, or hovercrafts. It is a region protected by the gods and goddesses. Not one human has ever set foot on the soil of the Tideless Abyss."

"Not even Brenn?" Erica asked.

"Brenn can go there because he shares my soul shard, but only if my dragon takes him. We have not had the time. Matters here keep us far too busy." Ciara sipped from her wine.

"If humans can't set foot there, then how can we all go?" Erica continued.

"I have contacted my father, King Brokig. He has given permission. It is a wise decision. I do not think Zohmes and Odoxon are able to do anything in the Tideless Abyss, but we must not underestimate their combined powers or forget that Zohmes is a god."

Erica snorted. "A fallen god."

"Nevertheless, a god, and allied with the most powerful sorcerer that has ever existed on Ierilia. Combined, they are to be feared," Ciara said patiently.

"I hope you are correct in surmising it is the absence of Niqine and the handmaidens that is behind this vegetation phenomena," Biryn told Ciara.

"I hope so, too. Rania has been silent. I will continue in my attempts to contact her."

Brenn took Ciara's hand in his. "So if your father gave permission for us to go to your home, what if the Tideless Abyss is discovered by a spaceship or flyer? What happens if someone uninvited sets foot on its soil?"

"It cannot be discovered. It is hidden by a shield of clouds, rendering it invisible to the human eye."

"Is it cold there? What do we wear?" Ivran inquired.

"It is always warm."

Biryn set his goblet on the table. "If everyone is finished?"

Ciara and Taylith began toward the door. Just before they

left for the courtyard to call out their dragons, Ciara turned. "Please leave your weapons behind. Only the four swords are allowed."

"Your Majesty, thank you for lunch. I will return to Brenn's estate now," Laura told the king.

"You are welcome. Thank you for assisting us on such short notice," Biryn responded.

Taylith, just on his way through the door, turned. "You can come with us, Laura."

"Are you sure?"

"Yes. Come along."

Biryn raised his eyebrows at Brenn, who laughed softly. "I see a romance blooming," he whispered to the king.

Ciara and Taylith zoomed through the sky until they were above the gray cloud bed. Biryn held Cylena tightly against him, though Ciara assured them they could not fall. A spell held them securely in place just below her graceful neck.

The two dragons flew side by side. Biryn glanced at Taylith, wishing he had the ability to shift into a dragon. It had to be a wonderful sensation to fly so high above the clouds, free as a bird. The dragon's blue scales glistened like sparkling gems in the suns' rays. No wonder they were called jewel dragons.

It didn't take long before they approached a thick bed of white clouds. He wondered why there was a volume of clouds so high above the cloud bed below them. It was an unusual phenomenon. The dragons flew into the moist air, but it disappeared quite suddenly.

"Oh my God. This can't be real. Floating islands?" Erica exclaimed behind him.

Biryn gasped, as did Cylena. Surrounded by pink puffy clouds, smaller islands and one other larger one, connected to a large island above them with what looked like thick vines. Waterfalls cascaded down to the other islands. One of the smaller islands held a tall statue of a beautiful woman, her hand held up, cradling a huge glass tree. The tree seemed lit from within, sending rainbow colors all around it to the various islands and the waterfalls. Below it stood an exotic golden temple.

"Wow and wow! It reminds me of the Statue of Liberty on Earth, except this statue is wondrous!" Erica said.

Brenn called out to them. "Ciara just told me. It is the goddess of beauty holding the tree of life. That is the temple where their people go to worship the gods and goddesses."

They closed in on the main island. It was wondrous to behold. A snow-white castle looked out over a sea of trees laden with pastel blossoms. Just below the castle, a waterfall cascaded from its foundation into a pristine, crystal-clear lake. Glass statues, one of a woman, the other of a man, flanked the waterfall. The statues were tall, reaching all the way up to the castle. They looked to be sculpted from crystal.

The dragons landed in the castle's courtyard, the floor smooth and shiny like glass. They slid down Taylith and Ciara's necks as they bent low for them, then they waited for the two dragons to change.

King Brokig and his queen approached. "Welcome to the Tideless Abyss."

Ciara flew into her mother's arms, then embraced her father. "Father, Mother, we do not have time to visit with you. You know why we are here."

"Yes. I have summoned Niqine and the handmaidens. They will be here soon." The king shook hands with all of them. "There was no need to bring the whole team. No one can harm us here," he told Biryn.

Biryn frowned. "Not entirely true. Cewrick managed to

change all your people into black dragons."

"With the help of the gods and goddesses, we have ensured that such a thing can never happen again."

Biryn shook his head. "Do not be too sure of that. Zohmes and Odoxon are in league. I am sure Ciara has told you?"

"Ciara has updated us on some events, yes, and I am happy you are fully recovered from the attack on your life. I fear for Niqine and the maidens returning to their home. Who is going to protect them from Zohmes and Odoxon?" Brokig questioned.

"Brokig, we have no choice. You know their habitat is close to Xynnar. All vegetation is dying. We fear it is because Niqine and the handmaidens are no longer there. I will send guards to watch over them."

"They have not lived there for centuries, as you know. Why would this happen now?" Brokig asked.

"The land senses that we are alive and well, and living here." Niqine suddenly appeared, joined the group, then bowed before the two kings.

"How is that possible? You have lived here with us since your release from the caves. Nothing can penetrate the containment spell." Brokig looked puzzled.

"There was a breach recently. Nothing happened, so I did not report it to you. I am sorry. I should have said something." Niqine sounded upset.

"How did you know about the breach?"

"Rania told me. It was a spell that only lasted seconds. The gods caught it right away and stopped it. There is an even stronger screen around the islands now, that, according to Rania, nothing can penetrate."

"This is how the land sensed your return and the location of you and the maidens?"

"I suspect that is what happened, but I am not sure."

"Did the goddess also tell you what caused the breach?"

"She did not know. She suspects Zohmes and Odoxon. I am so sorry, Your Majesty." A tear trickled down Niqine's golden cheek.

Biryn looked at the group of tiny, winged people. They were so petite, fragile, and beautiful. He was tempted to leave them where they were safe. *Do I want this responsibility?*

"Are you sure you want to leave here, Niqine?" Brokig asked.

"It must be as it is written. The maidens and I thank you for hiding us here and your help, but we cannot argue with the book of knowledge." She looked up at Biryn. "Your Majesty, our village has probably crumbled into piles of debris or turned to dust after being abandoned for so long. Where will we live?"

Ciara answered. "Niqine, Rania has assured me that your village is intact. She has shielded it from the elements. Everything should be as you left it, just like the Tideless Abyss was protected while the dragons were cursed."

Niqine looked relieved. "Thank the goddess. We are ready to return. I for one have missed our home greatly."

Ciara and Taylith stepped away from the group and shifted back to their dragons, both kneeling to allow the group to climb onto their backs. Once the dragons took off, it didn't take them long to fly to the valley. The view of Xynnar Valley from the sky showed a devastating picture. The trees and foliage looked diseased, much like his people were when the plague was released upon them. The land looked as if it were dying and it was spreading. Could this have gone on longer than any of them suspected? By the gods, he hoped the return of Niqine and Rania's handmaidens would repair the damage done to the area.

A few more beats of the dragons' wings brought them to

the mines and the ridge of mountains at the edge of the valley. Biryn held on to Cylena, and Ciara slowed and started her descent to the mountain peaks below them.

To Biryn's surprise, the handmaidens' domain was a small village well hidden within a crater in the center of one of the smaller mountain peaks. Exquisite buildings and a temple carved completely from crystal dotted the area, located near a small, vivid blue lake. He had seen the holographs of the castle Niqine was provided with when she was trapped within the crystal cave. The temple was an exact replica. More of the crystals jutted from the ground, forming elegant sculptures of the gods and goddesses. The area was lush with plant and wildlife, the statues and buildings surrounded by blooming flowers and elegant gardens. The magick of the village surrounded Biryn, sinking beneath his skin, invigorating him. It puzzled him that none of the vegetation within the crater was affected by the disease.

"We need to make sure the buildings are clear. I don't want any surprises," Aldis warned.

"You, Brenn, Laro, and Ivran inspect the houses. Icaras and Cewrick will investigate the temple in case there is some unforeseen magick, but from the power I feel protecting the village, I doubt it is necessary." Biryn gave Icaras a pointed look. "Keep your personal feelings aside. We need to ensure Niqine and the handmaidens' safety."

Biryn sighed in relief. No argument, no angry remark. All Icaras did was clench his jaw. Then he swiveled to join Cewrick to check the temple interior.

There were only fifteen Chihni, including Niqine, so the village was quite small. It didn't take the team long to make sure everything was secure. Aldis, Brenn, Ivran, and Laro returned to the group, followed by Icaras and Cewrick. Both men looked rattled.

Aldis gestured to the row of small homes. "The housing is clear."

Biryn caught Icaras' gaze. The man looked as though he had seen an apparition. "Is the temple safe?"

"Of course. Rania protects it."

"Then what has the both of you looking so troubled, besides the continued angst."

Cewrick stepped up beside Icaras and put his hand on his son's shoulder. Biryn was shocked that Icaras allowed his father to get near him, much less touch him. "It is the temple of Rania. A temple Hirsuta helped build for the priestess. Her essence can be felt throughout the temple."

Biryn didn't think that was the only thing that bothered Cewrick and Icaras, but obviously they did not want to discuss it out in the open. He would question them after their return to Cront and get to the bottom of the sudden change in their demeanor. Not that he would complain if Icaras could put his anger toward his father aside. Cylena hurried to her father and brother, along with Astiana and Ciara. He knew they hoped to calm them both.

He turned his attention to Brenn. "I would like Trevain's unit to provide protection for the Chihni. They could easily be trapped within the crater by Zohmes and Odoxon."

"Do not worry, Your Majesty. There is a network of tunnels below the city that will give us an escape route if Zohmes does try to enter the village. That is how I escaped Cewrick with the book of knowledge after he cursed the dragons," Niqine stated.

She may have escaped Cewrick that time, but Biryn wasn't taking any chances with their safety. "Nevertheless, the warriors will be placed here for your protection. I will tolerate no argument. Your safety is of utmost concern."

"Biryn, a hovercraft will not be able to land so close to the koriam mines, and from the looks of the temple, it is carved completely from koriam crystal," Brenn pointed out.

"If you will contact Trevain to have his warriors ready for departure, I will pick them up from your estate and bring them to the village," Taylith offered.

Brenn took out his communicator. "This may not work because of the koriam."

"Biryn, can I hitch a ride back with Taylith? That way I can stop by the compound to see Barry before it gets late." Erica twisted her face in a grimace. "I would like to get that meeting done and over with. He can be a pain in the ass to deal with, especially since he thinks he is still in charge of my people."

Hitch a ride...okay, he understood that one...and pain. That, too. "Pain in the ass?" Erica's phrases made no sense most of the time, but he had to admit he was growing fond of a few of her terms, especially when it was an endearment uttered from his sweet Cylena's lips.

"An obnoxious person...like Ivran, except Barry is so much worse. Using pain in the ass is much too nice for him."

Ivran grimaced. "Stop choosing me for your examples, Erica."

Biryn shook his head and laughed. "Take care of it, but make sure he understands that he will not have a position of power over your people as he did on Earth. After researching the data of your government, I do not trust him to lead your people in any manner. The Earth people can vote for a leader, but after they begin building."

Laura stood beside Erica. "I'll go with Erica and Taylith. Julia is staying at the compound, and I would like to check on her."

Brenn closed his communicator and put it in his pocket. "I managed to contact Trevain. He is readying his unit and will be waiting at my estate. Erica, Garnoc has been notified to take you and Laura to the compound upon your arrival. We will meet back at my estate after Trevain arrives."

"This will be a short flight." Taylith moved to a clear area and shifted to his dragon, then knelt for Erica and Laura to climb onto his back.

Erica opened the door to the compound and stepped inside. Laura, walking closely behind her, grabbed her arm and pulled her into an empty room.

"You were with them when they rescued Cewrick, but you didn't think to tell me or Mark? The wizard was at the joining ceremony, for God's sake." Laura's voice hitched.

Erica's heart twisted. Would Laura believe her if she told her the truth? Icaras was having a hard time believing it, why would Laura? "Oh, honey, I know I should have told you, but I didn't know if you would believe me. Zohmes possessed Cewrick for centuries. His essence entered Cewrick moments before Icaras and Cylena were born. He didn't torture you or Mark. It was Zohmes."

Pain filled Laura's eyes. "Taylith told me. He also told me that he was with you when you rescued Cewrick from Zohmes and Odoxon. All of you were." She rubbed her face. "I just wish you would have confided in me."

Erica pulled her into her arms and hugged her friend tightly. "I am so sorry, Laura. You're right. I should have told both you and Mark right after the rescue. When we get back to Brenn's estate, I will tell him. But understand, the being that tortured you was not Cewrick."

Laura hugged her back, then stepped out of her arms. "I know he wasn't. The man that tortured me was much older, his face twisted with anger, and his eyes were full of hatred. I could almost see the flames of rage flickering in them. He was a monster. The Cewrick I saw today was not that man. This man has a world of pain troubling him. I secretly studied him, his facial expressions, his eyes especially. He comes across as kind and compassionate." She took a deep breath. "Mark already knows. I made Taylith tell him after he warned me that Cewrick would be at the palace with you. He is upset that you kept this from us. After Mark sees and meets Cewrick, he will know the truth, just as I do."

Erica's communicator went off. She pulled it from her pocket and, after looking at the screen, answered it.

It was Barry. "Erica, it is well past afternoon. I am waiting in the commons area for our meeting."

Erica poked her tongue out at the communicator. "I will be there in less than five minutes." She closed it and stuck it back into her pocket. "I had better go and meet with him before he drives me nuts."

Laura laughed. "Better you than me. I don't like that man. He gives me the creepy crawlies, and to think he was supposed to be our leader gives me shivers down my spine."

They left the room and walked toward the commons area. When they reached it, Laura turned to head to her sister's room.

"Bring Julia here. I'd like to see her, too," Erica called out after her, then opened the door.

She couldn't believe her eyes. It was almost as if she were back home on Earth at the barracks before they had left on their mission. Twinkling lights hung from the ceiling, along with handmade stars. Wreaths made from evergreens, decorated with bows in reds and golds, graced the walls. Candle holders on the tables, with elegant bows tied around their base, stood nestled in the center of a smaller wreath of the same greenery. In the far corner of the room stood a tree, decorated with handmade ornaments, bows, and the same kind of lights that hung from the ceiling. Her crew had brought Christmas to Ierilia, and it was breathtaking.

"Wow. Christmas on Ierilia," she exclaimed. "When is our Christmas party?"

"Erica, please have a seat. We do not have time for you to admire the decorations and think about parties."

Erica turned at the sound of Barry's voice. The man really grated on her nerves. She walked to the table and sat down.

"First, about this realm the king has given us. Do you know where it is located? How many survivors do we have on the planet? I must get them together to form a plan of action to move forward with our mis—"

Erica interrupted him. "Barry, I know you were placed in charge when we left Earth, but there is no longer a mission, and you are not in charge. We crash-landed on an inhabited planet. The king has been kind enough to take us in, provide us with food, clothing, and shelter. He even granted us our own realm with the promise to help us build a city. We now fall under their customs and their rules."

Barry gave her a penetrating stare. "I was chief of staff to the president. I am in charge of this mission."

Erica did not back down and would not allow Barry to push her or their crew around. "No, Barry. You are not in charge of anything. On this planet you are nothing. You have no rank, no power. It will be up to the crew members to decide who will lead our people. Here, there will be no government, no president, no vice president, no chief of staff. I don't know if you were trained for anything else but politics, but I'm sure you can learn some kind of trade. There are no politics on Ierilia. Crimes are judged by the gods, goddesses, and the king, so there is no need for lawyers. On Ierilia, each realm has one ruler. Those rulers fall under the king's rule. When we start building, we will hold a vote. That person will deal directly with the king, as is customary on Ierilia. We have also started a suggestion list for a name for our realm. The datapad is over there on that small table against the wall. If you have any ideas for a name, feel free to add it to the list."

"This is outrageous. Captain Martinez, you are stripped of your rank, and I am immediately placing you under arrest for insubordination."

Laughter erupted around them. Several members of the crews had entered the room.

"Barry, I would like to see you try to strip Erica of her rank." Bernie walked to the table, Gordon beside him.

Gordon winked at Erica, then told Barry, "She is a high-ranking captain in the king's army. You would do well to watch your tongue. She may have to send you to the stockade."

"She wouldn't dare."

Erica gave him a hard stare. "Yes, Barry, I *would* dare. Each captain oversees their respective crews while living in the compound. You are a crewmember only and will follow the instructions given you by your captain. You can speak with any of the liaisons if you have questions. Mark is the head liaison and reports directly to me."

Barry stood up and briskly left the room. It was obvious he wasn't happy with the situation, but like the rest of them, he would have to learn to live on Ierilia and follow its laws and customs.

"Thanks, Gordon…Bernie. He can be a jerk to deal with. I remember his high-handed attitude when we were training."

Gordon grinned at her. "Don't worry about Barry. We'll keep him straight."

"Erica, it is good to see you," Julia said, taking a seat at the table. Laura sat down beside her.

Erica didn't miss the change in Julia's demeanor. Since John had been killed and Zohmes left his body, she was no longer pushing her sister away and seemed to be settling in well. "Julia, how are you feel—"

Both Erica and Laura's communicators went off. "Garnoc," they said at the same time.

"I'm sorry, our ride is here." Erica looked at Julia. "Would you like to come to Brenn's estate with us for dinner? It will give you a chance to spend a little more time with Laura."

Julia smiled timidly. "I'd love to."

They said goodbye to the others that had filed into the room. Erica took a last look at the decorations and Christmas tree. Just for a little while, it had almost felt like she was back on Earth. Not that she felt homesick. Not at all. But the Christmas holidays were always sort of special. It would be nice to continue that traditional holiday on Ierilia. While they left the building, she said, "You know, it might be snowing, but we have no clue what month it is. Time is calculated so differently here, and Christmas celebrates the birth of Christ. So how do we decide if this is the right month?"

Laura nodded. "I know. We've talked about it and decided we'll celebrate it this month and keep it that way. Many of us were raised as Christians. We would like to continue the tradition as best we can."

"That would be nice. Apparently, there are celebrations here to honor their gods and goddesses, though Lord knows when. We've hardly had time. Hell, it was hard enough to find time for the weddings. I'm sure you've both learned their calendars. There are sixty-two days in a month, and they have fourteen months in a year. Laro told me this is the month of frost. That kind of goes with Christmas."

"We still need to draw names for Christmas gifts and

decide on an evening for the party." Julia suddenly stopped and held her belly.

"What's wrong?" Erica studied Julia's pain-filled eyes.

"I don't know. Some weird spasms I've been getting. They hurt."

"You need to see Catrice." Laura took Julia's arm.

"Not today. I'm okay. It's gone again."

Erica was more concerned than she showed. Was little Satan causing problems for Julia?

CHAPTER TWENTY-ONE

Biryn slid off Ciara's back and held his arms out for Cylena as she glided to the ground. They had stayed in Niqine's village long enough for Trevain and his unit of twelve warriors to settle in and set up a watch cycle. Most of them were engineered men, but not all. Trevain had made sure to bring some of their technological equipment, but with so many of the koriam crystals around them, there was no guarantee any of it would function. If something happened, it was possible they wouldn't find out about it until one of the warriors could make it out of the valley to contact them. He still felt uneasy about Niqine and the maidens and their return to their home. Even with the assurance of protection by the gods and goddesses, and Trevain and his unit in place, he could not shake the feeling that something was off.

He shivered and hurried Cylena along. Snow continued to fall steadily, and they had not worn warm clothing. He was glad when they entered Brenn's house and found a big crackling fire in the huge fireplace warming the living area and dining room.

He gratefully accepted a glass of eldalas spirit. Brenn offered the women wine, except Julia. "I will ask Gieth for milk for you," he told her.

"Before the others join us, Icaras, Cewrick, when you returned from the temple of the Chihni, you both seemed troubled, and your faces were as white as the snow outside. Please tell us what you saw inside?" Biryn looked at both men.

Cewrick answered him in a voice laced with emotion. "Icaras and I shared the same vision. It was of Hirsuta. She is held captive on Wuits Peak in Odoxon's cave. He now resides in his castle, so she is alone. He has chained her to the cave wall. She has some straw for a bed. She was naked but so caked with dirt and filth, I hardly recognized her. Her body is covered with sores and wounds. Her hair hangs to her feet. She uses it to try and cover her nakedness. Vermin crawled all around her, several gnawing on her bloodied feet. Blood dripped from—"

"Father, stop!" Icaras yelled.

Biryn set his glass on the low table next to him. "I have heard enough. Now that we know she is alive and where, we can plan to rescue her."

"I fear for her," Icaras whispered, tears escaping from beneath his downcast eyelids. "She is barely alive. I feel ill at the memory of what we saw."

"She has suffered centuries of torture and abuse. Brenn? Aldis?" Biryn looked at them for advice.

Ciara answered instead. "I will go to the study. I hope Rania can give us guidance."

"No one can scale that mountain. That is why he was banished to that cave." Brenn drank his eldalas in one gulp.

"How did she even survive all those centuries? With no food, no water. It is unbelievable," Cylena said in a tremulous voice.

"How did Hirsuta get there? With Zohmes' help of course. He has probably been providing the sorcerer with food and water for centuries and then spirited Hirsuta to the cave. We are dealing with two powerful entities now that Odoxon has his powers back. Rescuing Hirsuta will not be a simple task." Cewrick took Icaras' shaking hands in his.

To Biryn's surprise, Icaras allowed it. Trying to talk to Icaras had proven hopeless. Attempting to help mellow his anger toward his father had seemed almost futile. Their shared vision of mate and mother had accomplished the impossible. It had brought the two together, had mended the huge gap between them. The bad memories would fade over time.

Ciara returned and interrupted his musings.

"I was able to contact Rania. The goddess is overwhelmed with joy that her daughter is alive. She told me we must proceed with haste. Odoxon has neglected her since his departure from the cave. She has no water or food and is waning fast. She cannot die at their hands, but the lack of sustenance has already taken its toll on her. She is very weak and could easily slip into a deep slumber from which it will be difficult to awaken her. To save her will not be easy. Odoxon and Zohmes have created a giant and a monster to guard the peak and the cave. The giant will be difficult to defeat. There are also urcals flying around the peak. The four swords must go. Cewrick, your powers will be necessary. Icaras must accompany you as well."

Laro jumped up from his chair. "If Erica has to go, then I will go with her. I will not allow her to go alone."

Ciara hushed him. "Some of you will need to remain here to guard the queen and the others."

"She is my mother. I want to go," Cylena shouted.

"No. You cannot go. In your condition, you need to be very careful." Ciara sent her a warning look.

"Condition? I am fine."

Ciara smiled. "Cylena, you are carrying the heir to the throne under your heart."

Biryn almost fell off his chair. He looked at Cylena, shocked. "Already? You did not tell me."

"Biryn, I knew not until now. I am as surprised as you."

Ciara continued. "We will leave at sunup. Wear your protective warming suits. It will be very cold so high up. As you know, Wuits Peak is the highest on all of Ierilia. Flyers and hovercrafts cannot go there. Our dragons will take you."

Julia interrupted. "I wish I could participate in all this, but like Cylena, I can't. I don't feel well. Please excuse me so I can go and lie down in Laura's room? Maybe I should return to the compound. I'm not really hungry."

Laura instantly began to fuss over her sister. She looked at Biryn. "Maybe it's better she goes back? I'll go with her, seeing I'm not involved in this mission. Is that okay?"

Biryn nodded his assent. "I hope you feel better soon, Julia. I learned that the first months are the most difficult."

Inwardly, he worried about the infant growing within Julia. It was Zohmes' spawn. He might have used John as a host, but nevertheless, Zohmes' essence had seeded into the unborn child. *Zohmes is my great-grandfather. That means the infant is related to me.* He shook the thought away. "Let us eat. I see dinner on the tables in the dining room. We will leave at first light."

Biryn gathered Cylena into his arms. "My sweet queen, we are going to become parents."

"So Rania tells us. If I am carrying our infant, it is very early, Biryn. Are you happy?"

"Yes, my love. Are you?"

"Of course. I did not expect it to happen so soon, but now that I know, I am overjoyed."

He kissed her tenderly. "You need to take good care of yourself. No more missions for my queen."

"I hate that I cannot go with you. But your mission today involves my mother and I so want to go with you. I still cannot believe she is alive."

"She is. And I must hasten to meet with the others. Take care of yourself and our son."

Cylena giggled. "Maybe a daughter?"

"Ciara said heir, not heiress."

"True. Come home to me safely, my king."

After kissing her again, he got out of bed and quickly dressed. He had begun leaving clothing at Brenn's estate because he never knew if they were departing from there or from the palace.

Glancing at Cylena, he noticed she'd drifted off to sleep again. He felt so much love for her, and now she was carrying his son or daughter. The gods and goddesses had been kind to him. After taking his sword out of the safe, he hurried out of the room and to the kitchens, where they had agreed to meet. They were all ready and waiting for him.

"Biryn. We are all here now. Taylith and I will go to the courtyard and call out our dragons. All of you, meet us there." Ciara hurried out, accompanied by Taylith.

They gathered in the courtyard near the dragons. It was a smaller group this time. Brenn, Ciara, Taylith, Erica, Icaras, Cewrick, Laro, and himself. Were there enough of them to defeat whatever monster Odoxon and Zohmes had guarding the cave?

With three of them on each dragon, they flew off to Wuits Peak. Biryn could not help but think about Cylena and the infant she carried. Would she be in more danger now from Zohmes? They had to keep her condition a secret as long as possible. Then again, Zohmes seemed to know everything.

Had he possessed another body? Was he walking among them? It scared him. He had never suspected Raollin. Zohmes had managed to possess the personal aide he had trusted with his life. And Erica had been fooled by John, one of her Earth crew. He shook his head to clear his mind. Right now, he needed to concentrate on Hirsuta's rescue.

He was glad when they rose above the snow and the gray cloud bed. The higher they flew, the colder it got, but his skin suit kept him toasty warm. Laro and Erica sat behind him. Brenn, Icaras, and Cewrick flew with Ciara. Like earlier, when he had admired Taylith's dragon, he now beheld Ciara's beauty. Her mauve-and-purple dragon scales shone in the suns' rays like jewels. She had to be the most beautiful of all dragons. Taylith and Ciara's gossamer-fine wings flapped steadily, barely making a sound. He was, as always, amazed at their speed. They could fly as fast, if not faster, as his spaceships.

Wuits Peak appeared in the distance. It was so high, it rose above the cloud bed. Dark specks surrounded the peak. They had to be the urcals. What looked like a rock formation stood atop the peak.

As they flew closer, he noticed it was not a rock formation. It was the giant. They approached steadily. The giant stood still as if hewn out of the stone below him. Was it even alive? The monstrous man did not move at all, not even when they were almost close enough to the cave's mouth to land.

They faced the cave now, the landing barely big enough for one dragon to set down and shift. Ciara landed first and called out her human. Biryn shivered at the sight of the cave's entrance. It was the mouth of a giant skull. Jagged teeth projected from it. Its hollow black eye sockets seemed to gaze down at the intruders. Craggy stone steps led up to the monstrous entrance.

Biryn had barely slid down and set foot on the landing, and Taylith had just changed into his human, when the stone beneath his feet shook as if the peak protested. One huge foot stepped down from the top of the peak, then another. The giant lifted a foot, ready to trample them. Biryn looked up. The thing was huge, and grossly distorted. What kind of imagination had created such a contorted being? It had the body of a man, but its skin seemed like granite, its muscles grotesque. One claw-like hand with pointy black nails held a stone mallet the size of a building. The other hand raised a flaming sword. Where there should be nipples, two big round red eyes shifted from side to side. On its head were the largest horns he'd ever seen, with two more horns protruding from its neck. Spikes adorned its shoulders and arms down to the wrists that had snake-like creatures slithering around them. The thing roared. Biryn clapped his hands over his ears and jumped aside as a fat monster foot attempted to trample them.

"How do we defeat this thing?" he shouted.

Cewrick raised his hands and chanted. Fiery lightning shot from his fingers. It bound the giant's legs but otherwise did no harm to it.

Icaras and Ciara joined Cewrick in his chant. Biryn ran to Erica and Taylith. The two stood helplessly watching, their swords held high, ready to attack. Laro and Brenn had called out their lions and were busy on the steps, fighting a creature three times their size. The growls were deafening, echoing back at them from the cave, the giant's roars shaking the peak. It swung its flaming sword in a circle above its head, then crashed it down toward the chanting sorcerers. Shafts of red lightning shot upward. Just in time flaming tendrils curled around the arm and stopped it mid-air. As the mallet came down toward them, Cewrick, Icaras, and Ciara joined hands, their faces raised, their chant so loud it overpowered the giant's roar. The mallet crumbled into dust. Particles rained down upon them.

"It is impossible!" Biryn shouted.

"The swords!" Ciara yelled. "Brenn, we need you here!"

Brenn changed. He ran to join them. Erica, Taylith, Biryn, and Brenn pointed their swords and touched. A shaft of bright white light shot up from the swords' points straight up at the giant's head. A loud roar. The peak seemed to sway when the monster man began to disintegrate.

A large pile of dust now lay where the giant had stood just seconds ago.

Brenn looked back at Laro's lion, still attempting to fend off the monster that guarded the entrance. "What do we do with that?" he called out.

"Your lions cannot best it. These creatures are not made of flesh and bone. Hold the swords together again pointing at it, and follow us." Cewrick motioned for Ciara and Icaras to advance. They walked slowly toward the creature while chanting.

Just like with the giant, a shaft of light issued from the swords directly at the monster. It, too, crumbled to dust and rubble.

Biryn wiped the sweat off his brow. Cewrick started up the steps, with Icaras hot on his heels, but Ciara stopped them. "Wait. Throw your swords at those teeth."

They threw the swords. Only two of them touched a stone tooth, but it was enough. Gleaming sharp metal spikes crashed down from the top of the entrance. They would have pierced anyone attempting to enter.

"Now we can go in, but slowly. We do not know what waits inside." Ciara stepped toward the opening and waved her hand at the steel spikes, causing them to bend enough for them to move through them.

Biryn gingerly walked through the opening behind Cewrick and Icaras and picked up his sword, the others following.

It took a moment for their eyes to adjust to the dim interior. Sconces on the walls held burning torches, their flames sending eerie shadows over the walls.

"It is exactly what we saw in the vision," Icaras told them.

Biryn walked slowly forward. A round black crystal sphere sat on a pedestal in the center of the cave. Large, leather-bound old books were piled high against the walls. Animal skins lay on the stone floor. An altar hewn from stone stood further down. On it, large candelabras held burned out black candles. A huge leather-bound book lay opened upon it. Vials and glass containers surrounded the book. "What is that book?" Biryn wondered.

"It is an ancient book of spells that Odoxon stole centuries ago. In the hands of the wrong sorcerer, it can do a lot of harm. I am surprised he left it here. It indicates he plans to come back. We will take it with us." Ciara had a worried look on her face.

"I have never seen so many real books except in the treasury," Biryn uttered. "All his powers were stripped from him for centuries. What would the sorcerer want with all the books and potions? They would do him no good."

"He did not want anyone else to have the books. He had to have had Zohmes' help in transporting them from his castle. Like I said before, I think Zohmes has been helping him all these centuries as a last resort. Zohmes restored his powers after we defeated Cewrick. He needed another ally. No matter how dangerous Odoxon is, it is all he has now."

"Where is my mother?" Icaras said anxiously.

They were about to advance to find her when they were blinded by a fierce orange light. A figure appeared.

"Odoxon," Biryn hissed.

Pure evil gazed at him, the eyes alight with fire. Biryn took the sorcerer's appearance in at a glance. The face was so old, it looked like parchment, the skin yellowed and severely creased. Wild yellowish hair hung to his waist, his beard almost to the ground. He wore a black robe, a black cloak draping from his shoulders. In his gnarled fingers he clasped a black staff topped by a black crystal skull that emitted an orange glow.

"You shall not take her!" For such an old being, the sorcerer had a mighty voice. He held up his staff.

Cewrick stepped forward. "No, old man! You cannot hurt my people!"

Cewrick's golden staff appeared magically in his hand. Biryn gasped as its red jeweled top began to glow. Cewrick swung it back and forth. The red jewel glowed brighter and brighter, fighting the flames issuing from Odoxon's staff. "You will not stop us, monster that you are!"

Icaras stepped toward the old sorcerer. With a motion of his staff, Odoxon sent him flying against the wall, causing books to come tumbling down.

"You will hurt my son? Take this!" Cewrick chanted a few foreign words and pointed his staff at Odoxon, crashing him to the stone floor.

"Go and find your mother!" Cewrick shouted at Icaras, who had scrambled up and moved toward the sorcerer again.

"Cewrick, you need us and —" Ciara began.

"No. Go help Icaras. I will deal with this lunatic!"

Biryn followed Ciara as she gingerly stepped around the two sorcerers. They had to advance far into the cave before they finally found Hirsuta. She appeared to be unconscious.

Ciara hurried to her and knelt by her side. Taking the vial of her tears from her pocket, she held it to Hirsuta's lips.

Biryn was shocked at the woman's appearance. Cewrick had described some of it, but seeing her now, it was worse than he had thought. Brenn draped his cloak over her to cover her nakedness. In a glance, Biryn had noticed Hirsuta's ribs almost poking through her skin. Ciara's tears started to take effect. Slowly, her eyes opened. Beautiful violet eyes, very close to the color of Ciara's, gazed at the group surrounding her.

"Who—"

Icaras knelt by his mother's side. "Mother…Mother…it is me. Icaras."

Hirsuta's parched lips attempted a smile. "My boy…" Her eyes closed again.

"She sleeps now, but it is a normal slumber. We were just in time," Ciara said. "Brenn, you will need to carry her."

"She is my mother. I will." Icaras began to pick her up.

"No. We still need to escape Odoxon. Your father is holding him but cannot defeat him. We may need your powers to help us." Ciara gently removed Icaras' hands from Hirsuta. "Allow Brenn or Laro to carry her."

"She weighs no more than a feather." Brenn wrapped his cloak tighter around Hirsuta and gathered her into his arms.

"Be careful," Biryn warned as he led the way back to the entrance.

Odoxon and Cewrick were still fighting. "We need to bind the old man," Biryn told Ciara.

Ciara shoved the spellbook into Erica's hands. "Yes. Taylith, take Erica, Laro, Brenn, and Hirsuta back to the palace. Hirsuta needs Catrice's care. The four of us should be able to bind Odoxon long enough for us to escape."

Biryn doubted he could be of any help. He might have his powers bestowed upon him, but he still had no idea how to use them.

"Come," Ciara told him and Icaras.

He followed her, his heart pounding as she advanced to stand behind Cewrick. From the corner of his eye, he saw Brenn and the others slip by and head out of the entrance.

"Noooooooo!" Odoxon roared and pointed his staff at the entrance.

"Now!" Ciara shouted and, grabbing his and Icaras' hand, began to chant, forcing Odoxon's staff down and turning it to point at himself instead.

Cewrick swiveled, grasped Icaras' free hand, and joined in the chant. The flapping of wings echoed into the cave. Taylith had successfully left Wuits Peak with his precious cargo.

Fury and hatred issued from Odoxon's eyes such as Biryn had never seen in his lifetime.

"Zohmes! Where in the gods' names are you!" Odoxon's shout echoed throughout the cave.

Biryn vaguely wondered about that himself. If Zohmes showed up, even with the four of them joining forces, there was no way they could get out of there. His lips automatically formed words. He had no idea how he could chant along, but he did.

A glowing red rope-like band snaked around Odoxon's body, binding his arms and staff to his sides. Still chanting, Cewrick urged the team toward the cave's entrance. Biryn felt some of the power flowing through him weaken as Ciara stepped away from them and called out her dragon.

Never breaking the chant, Cewrick, with Icaras holding his hand tightly so not to disrupt the spell, managed to get up on Ciara's leg and climb to her neck. Within seconds she shot up into the sky and flew away from the peak.

Biryn heaved a sigh of relief as he watched the peak disappear from sight.

CHAPTER TWENTY-TWO

Biryn stood at the door of the room in his small clinic and watched Cewrick, Icaras, and Cylena reunite with Hirsuta. Brenn had contacted Aldis and had asked him to bring the team to the palace to make sure Cylena was there when her mother arrived. Tears filled his eyes. He could only imagine what they had to be feeling right now. To find Hirsuta alive, after so many centuries, in the foul condition they had found her, reminded him of Cylena's imprisonment in Yanata. Horrified, he thought he would be sick. *By the gods, that could have been Cylena had they not been able to rescue her in time.*

Catrice and Jason had already worked wonders on Hirsuta. Except for her hair, she was clean. An IV attached to her hand was replenishing her fluids. Her blonde hair was still matted and dirty. Because of its length, they had to wrap it in a bundle above her head to keep it out of the way so they could work on her. Several of the wounds were so deep the bone was exposed, but those had been stitched. Hirsuta's wounds were extensive and would take time to heal, even with the help of Ciara's tears.

Ciara entered the infirmary, holding several large purple flowers. Biryn had been told they were the key to the antidote that had saved him. Now he prayed to the gods that those miraculous flowers would save Hirsuta as well.

Ciara held the flowers out to Catrice. "You will need to crush these into a paste. Hirsuta must ingest the flowers."

"Jason and I made a serum with the flowers for the veerveraine antidote. We can do the same with these. If you think it will work, I can administer the serum intravenously directly into the bloodstream."

Ciara nodded. "Do it. The serum will heal her quicker than ingesting them."

Catrice took the flowers to Jason in the lab. It felt as if only a few moments had passed, and she returned holding a vial and syringe. Biryn watched her hasten to Hirsuta's bedside, draw some of the fluid into the syringe, and inject the contents into the tubing. She repeated her actions until the vial was empty, then threw the needle and vial away.

Within moments of administering the medication, the wounds and bruises started to disappear. Hirsuta's skin now appeared flawless, though she was still very malnourished. Bones protruded from her thin limbs. It was a miracle she had survived as long as she had after Zohmes had freed Odoxon and they had abandoned her. Byrin thought because she was a child of the gods and goddesses, like him, nothing could really kill her. Though it was hard to imagine how anyone in her malnourished state could have survived at all.

Catrice checked her vitals and stepped away from the bed to join him. "I have no idea what is in those flowers of Ciara's, but the queen's mother is going to be just fine."

Suddenly, Hirsuta took a deep breath. She opened her eyes and tried to sit up. She looked frantic and began to struggle until the soothing voices of her children and mate calmed her. Cylena tucked the blankets back around her, and Icaras placed another pillow behind her back, allowing her to sit up.

Cewrick held her hand and wiped her brow with a damp cloth.

Hirsuta's hand flew to her mouth when her gaze traveled between Cylena, Icaras, and Cewrick. Sobs began to wrack her body, and tears streamed down her face. She shook her head as if she couldn't believe what was before her eyes. "How?"

Biryn rubbed tears off his face. The sight of them nearly broke him. The cruelty the family had faced for centuries was indescribable. He longed to take Cylena in his arms, to join her in the reunion, but he refused to intrude on their intimate moment. "Catrice, let Cylena know that we have returned to my chambers. I do not want to disturb them." He turned to the others and motioned for them to follow. "Let us allow them some privacy."

Biryn led the group back to his private chambers. Once inside, they seated themselves at his dining table. Dunmore had ordered a meal to be delivered and poured them each a glass of wine.

"Is the queen's mother going to be all right?" Dunmore inquired.

Biryn took a drink of his wine. "Yes, I believe she will. Thank you, Dunmore."

A few moments later, the staff arrived and placed food on the table. It was simple fare — sliced meats, cheese, bread, and fruit, but he didn't have much of an appetite after Hirsuta's rescue. He was sure the others didn't either.

Erica toyed with her glass, a look of contemplation on her face. "Hirsuta was in much worse shape than Laura and Mark were, and we had to take Cewrick to the Clyss to heal him. Will the flowers be enough to heal her completely?"

Ciara tucked a lock of hair behind her ear. "Her body will heal. The malnourishment will take longer, but I fear her mind and soul will take a very long time. The flowers can only heal physical damage. When she is well enough, we will take her to the Clyss."

Erica shook her head. "I don't think there is anything that can fix the mental and internal anguish she must be feeling."

"With the love of her mate and children, Hirsuta will heal in time."

The door opened, drawing Biryn's attention. He stood when Cylena, Icaras, and Cewrick entered, and he pulled a chair out for Cylena to sit. Cewrick and Icaras sat across from them. Dunmore poured them each a glass of wine.

"How is your mother doing?" he asked Cylena after he sat back down.

Cylena clasped his hand and squeezed. "She is sleeping now. Catrice said her wounds are healed, but she will need to stay in the infirmary for several days or at least until she is no longer dehydrated and is able to eat food other than soups."

Cewrick looked at each of them, his eyes glistening with unshed tears. "I would like to thank all of you for what you have done for my family. You have risked your lives to help each one of us, and I do not know how I will ever repay you for reuniting us."

Noise filled the room when Erica's communicator sounded off. She pulled it from her pocket and answered it. "Hi, Gordon. How is everything at the compound?"

"Erica, I don't know what in the hell is going on. I have Barry locked up in a storage closet."

Erica pulled a face and sounded exasperated. "Okay, Gordon, slow down. I am with the king, and I have you on speaker. Why do you have Barry locked up?"

Gordon started speaking in a rush. "It was crazy, Erica! Everyone was in the commons room, singing Christmas carols. Julia felt a little better, so she decided to join in. She was sitting off to the side, and Barry came in and kind of stood behind her. One minute they were both there and the next this black smoky stuff started coming out of Barry's ears and mouth. It surrounded Julia in some kind of fire tornado, then disappeared. It took Julia with it!"

"Gordon, did anyone else see what happened?"

"No, I don't think so. They were in a corner in the back behind everyone. I recorded it all on my datapad."

"Keep Barry locked up. I will be at the compound shortly."

Erica closed the communicator and placed it in her pocket.

Taylith jumped up from the table, his chair hitting the floor. "I need to go pick up Laura."

Biryn motioned for him to go ahead. If his suspicions were correct, Laura was the dragon's lifemate, and she would need his support. His jaw clenched. "Aldis, you, Erica, and Laro go to the compound and take Barry into custody. I want the datapad confiscated as well."

Icaras stood up. "I will go with them. Someone will need to wipe Gordon's memories. There could be others that may have seen something. We need to be sure."

Just as they were leaving, Brenn's communicator went off. Biryn's gut twisted, a bad sense of foreboding settling deep within.

"General, we have a problem," Trevain said.

Brenn jabbed at the speaker button. "Speak up, Trevain."

"Niqine is gone."

"What?" Brenn yelled. "How?"

"She told the guards she wanted to go to the market. One of the guards said he would contact Taylith to fly her there and they had to wait on the edge of the crater. Several of the guards witnessed what happened next. The guard and Niqine stood waiting when suddenly smoke and flames began to pour out of the guard's mouth, nose, and ears. It enveloped

Niqine. It appeared to eat her. The possessed guard remembers nothing, and Niqine is completely gone. Vanished."

"We will be there shortly." Brenn almost threw his communicator on the table.

Biryn had jumped up. "Will that monster ever stop? By the gods! I had a feeling something was not right. It is why Zohmes was unavailable to help Odoxon. We know why he wants Niqine—for the book of knowledge. But what does he want with Julia?"

Ciara stood ready to fly Brenn to Xynnar. "She is carrying Zohmes' child."

"And after Julia delivers, he will keep little Satan and get rid of her. I should have kept a closer eye on her," Erica said.

Biryn put a finger to his lips, looking at Erica, but too late. Laura and Taylith walked back in. She had heard the last of the conversation. Her face had turned chalky white, and she held Taylith's arm in a death grip.

"What the hell do you mean? My sister is pregnant with the Antichrist? Oh my God! How is that even possible?"

COMING SOON

SHARD IN THE MIRROR

How does a dragon tell the woman he loves that it was he that had delivered her into the hands of the enemy?

Enslaved as one of Cewrick's feared black dragons, for centuries Taylith had been forced to do the evil sorcerer's bidding. Finally, free of the shackles of slavery, Taylith is enlisted by King Biryn as a member of his elite team.

Plagued with visions of an impending war and the return of the black dragon he once was, Taylith must find a way to tell his lifemate, Laura, that he was the creature that had captured her and delivered her into the hands of the enemy.

To keep Laura safe and save her sister from Zohmes' clutches, he must allow the god to change him back into the feared creature he once was.

EXCERPT

Taylith paced in front of the bedroom window while Laura readied herself for bed. Every feeling she had experienced slashed through him like a knife. The guilt of Julia's abduction, fear of and *for* the infant her sister carried, and the terror of what Zohmes may do to them both. They *should* be afraid of what Zohmes would and could do. *The infant is related to the king.* None of them had given a thought about who exactly the child was to Biryn. *Of course it all makes sense now. If we for some reason cannot rescue Julia, and Zohmes manages to keep the infant, he probably will raise him to rule Ierilia. Except no one knows yet that the queen has conceived. That will thwart the monster's plans when the news becomes public.*

He turned when the door of the bathroom opened. Laura stepped through, her long, blonde hair spilling around her shoulders. It had grown several inches since he had first set eyes on her, and he longed to thread his fingers through those silky strands. The nightdress she wore must have been part of her clothing from Earth. It came to just above her knees. It had a colored animal on the front much like a youngling's drawing. It had long ears, a pink nose and belly, and big feet. It was holding an axe behind its back. *How odd.* On her feet were pink fluffy shoes that had the same strange animal on them. He shook his head, trying to contain a laugh. How could she possibly look so delectable wearing such a thing?

She patted the animal on her nightshirt, while walking to stand before him. "What...it's Happy Bunny...see?" She pointed to the symbols below the picture. "Cute but psycho. Julia gave it to me when we were accepted into the relocation program."

"Psycho?"

She clasped his hands in hers, a hint of pain flashing in her green eyes. "Yes...just like my life right now. Everything has gone crazy and I feel helpless to stop it."

He pulled her into his arms and studied her face. Outwardly, she seemed to be calm, but he could still feel the tumult of emotions that raged within her. "We will find your sister. The gods will not allow him to keep her or the baby."

"Zohmes tortured and almost killed me. I couldn't bear it if he does the same to Julia." She slid her arms around his neck. "I can't stand to think about it anymore." Standing on her tiptoes, she kissed him, tentatively at first, then forcing his lips apart, passionately.

It was a demand he did not have the power to ignore. The feel of her in his arms, the sweet taste of her lips, ignited a fire within him that could not be quenched. From the moment he had seen her at Ciara's betrothal celebration, he had hungered for her. He had known who she was, what he had done to her. All the time fighting his attraction, he kept his distance. He had no wish to hurt her more than he already had. Each time he had seen her, that connection within him grew stronger, weakening his resolve. When Ciara had asked him to stay at Brenn's estate to protect Laura and the others, he had gladly left the Tideless Abyss just to be near her. He dug his fingers into the sleek softness of her hair while claiming her lips. His hands glided down her back to cup the cheeks of her shapely ass. Lifting her from the floor, he carried her to her bed, gently lowering her onto the soft comforter.

She pulled him down beside her, her lips seeking his, her hands trailing down his chest to the waist of his pants. She whispered, "God, Taylith, I need to forget about tonight."

Taylith stilled, his sanity clawing back to the surface through his passion-soaked mind. He wanted nothing more than to lose himself in her arms, but not when pain was the driving force of her need. He kissed her gently on the cheek and took a deep breath to calm his desire, willing his needy cock to behave. "I cannot, Laura. Not like this."

Laura flopped onto her back on the bed. "Why not? Most men would jump at the chance to have sex, especially with no strings attached."

After spending time with both Laura and Erica, he understood several of their Earth terms, sex was one of them, and he refused to mate with her just for the sake of it. He gazed down at her beautiful face and reached out to caress her cheek. "Because I will not be a tool to help you forget everything that has happened and to ease your pain." He teased her bottom lip with his fingertip and fought the urge to nip it with his teeth. "Because I want more than you are ready to give."

"Like what?" she murmured while tugging at the string at the top of his pants.

He gently took her hand and placed it on his chest. "Laura, we have become very close."

She toyed with the laces of his tunic, pulling several free. "Yes. Besides Julia, you are my best friend. Almost like the big brother I never had."

Best friend? Brother? He groaned inwardly. "What if I want to be more than a friend or brother? And do brothers and sisters mate on Earth?"

She giggled. "No, brothers and sisters do not mate. That's just disgusting." She maneuvered her fingers beneath the material of his tunic to caress his chest. "But *friends* sometimes do. It's called friends with benefits."

He tenderly stroked her face, then, playing with her hair, looked down into her eyes. "My sweet, I understand your need, but what drives it is your troubled mind and soul. What you want will give you a brief respite only. Like I said before, I desire more than that. You are more precious to me than you realize."

"I value our friendship, Taylith." She uttered a long sigh. "Just stay with me, then? Hold me?"

There was that word again. *Friendship.* After she relaxed on the pillows, he lay beside her and took her into his arms.

Stroking her hair, he watched her eyelids finally droop. Tenderly cradling her, he wished she returned his feelings. But it was too soon. In a way he felt relieved. He wanted her heart, her soul, her love, but if and when the time came for her to reciprocate his desires, he would have to tell her the truth. For now, he would have to be satisfied with friendship and camaraderie. Still pondering on his dilemma, he drifted off into a restless slumber.

BOOKS IN THIS SERIES:

In Search of Pride – Book 1

The Dragon's Lion – Book 2

Sword of Betrayal – Book 3

Sword of Judgement – Book 4

Testing the Crown – Book 5

Coming Soon:

Shard in the Mirror – Book 6

Initiation Genesis – Book 7

Tabeka's Revenge – Book 8

Infinite Fury – Book 9

The Lion's Stowaway and The Frozen Portal – novellas set in the Crimson Realm series.

ABOUT THE AUTHORS

Taryn Jameson

Taryn Jameson is a mother, grandmother, artist, and avid reader who lives in an enchanted forest that sparks her imagination to create. Her latest outlet is the written word. She is the alter ego of cover artist Angela Waters.

Gabriella Bradley

Gabriella Bradley has been a writer and artist all her life, though only ventured into erotic works in 2003. Her hobbies include art, gardening, swimming, sewing, embroidery. Favorite movies are old timers like Gone with the Wind, Spartacus, etc. Favorite music is Abba. All-time favorite series is Fringe.